TRISKAIDEKAPHOBIA

And Other Noir Tales

Also by Roger Keen

THE MAD ARTIST:
Psychonautic Adventures
in the 1970s

LITERARY STALKER

THE EMPTY CHAIR

MAN OF LETTERS

TRISKAIDEKAPHOBIA

And Other Noir Tales

ROGER KEEN

Darkness Visible

Published by Darkness Visible 2023

First published in Great Britain in 2023
by Darkness Visible Publishing

www.dv-publishing.com

ISBN 978-1-9998516-5-1

'Triskaidekaphobia' was previously published in *Psychotrope*; 'North' in *Threads*; 'All The King's Horses' in *Sierra Heaven*; and '*Real* Horror' in *Miskanthropic*.

For Andy

Contents

Introduction   1

Triskaidekaphobia   3

The Runner   15

North   20

Caught in the Labyrinth   25

All the King's Horses   49

The Photographer   54

Real Horror   77

Whiteout   94

The Empty Chair Chapter 1.   118

Introduction

These stories were all written in the early to mid-1990s, a period where I had left behind the uncompleted novels of the previous decade and had decided to be more pragmatic, producing shorter work that I would hopefully get published in magazines. I aimed for a particular section of the market that could best be described as 'dark' or 'noir' fiction, including borderline horror and crime elements but retaining a footing in 'literary' fiction, and sometimes veering into black comedy. The eight stories here represent favourites from around thirty to forty that I produced, and some of the more obviously 'genre' pieces did appear in magazines of the era, including *Sierra Heaven*, *Psychotrope*, *Threads* and *Flickers 'n' Frames*, as did my concurrent non-fiction work.

Looking back, I can see early examples of experimentation with different voices and modes of narration that was continued in my work of the 2000s onwards. And having written about 'the past' – meaning my experienced past – so extensively in *The Mad Artist* and *The Empty Chair*, I find work here that is contiguous with a past or historical present, one that doesn't differ greatly from the actual present, apart from in the area of technology. So, the stories could be contemporary, except where absence of wide personal use of computers and mobile phones comes to bear, together with photography, which still involved chemicals and celluloid negatives, and the now strangely atavistic practice of smoking in pubs and bars. Also, when it comes to sex, the fear of AIDS was much higher then, as was the fear of Creutzfeldt–Jakob disease when eating beef products. All these elements pop up in the stories as reminders of another zeitgeist.

As the '90s moved on, my commitment to short stories declined somewhat, and my ideas tended to be more 'literary' and less 'genre'. What this meant was an increasing struggle to get them published, as the majority of indie press magazines had specific genre requirements. One editor suggested that I 'improve' a story about political intrigue by turning the characters into vampires and succubae, but the idea seemed ridiculous. Eventually the well of story ideas became exhausted, and after the mid-'90s I never penned another, my ideas channelling into extended writing instead. So, this collection hangs together as all of a piece, a time capsule, a kind of curiosity to be encased and sent off into space…

Also included is Chapter 1. of my second novel *The Empty Chair*, which is the apotheosis of my fiction to date, and the eventual destination of the tendencies in these stories. Published in 2021, it relates the story of Steve Penhaligon and his journey through psychotherapy and TV direction from the 1980s onwards, culminating in the creation of a cinematic 'fairy tale of psychotherapy'…which is not all it seems…

TRISKAIDEKAPHOBIA

Bad things happen in association with the number thirteen. I've tested the situation and found this to be empirically true. On my thirteenth birthday I fell off my racing bike birthday present and broke one of my front teeth. On the thirteenth of last month a car with thirteen in its registration number nearly killed me on a zebra crossing, then the driver had the cheek to give me the finger, as though it was *my* fault! I could go on; the list is interminable. As well as fairly major incidents like these, my days are punctuated by scores of minor mishaps – making a mistake at thirteen minutes past the hour, tripping on the stairs approaching floor thirteen of a building, reading something disturbing on page thirteen of a newspaper...But all of these things put together amount to nothing – absolutely nothing – compared to what happened when I encountered Alison: The Thirteenth Girl.

It came about when Simon – a close friend and fellow student at Bristol University – invited me to his birthday party at his home in Kingston-Upon-Thames. Simon comes from a moneyed background; his big birthday bash is a regular event, and he wasn't breaking with tradition just because he was away studying. So, late on the appointed afternoon, nine of us piled into two cars and tore off down the M4, my contingent passing a bottle of tequila back and forth as we went. Unsurprisingly, the mood was highly exuberant, and from my own peculiar standpoint I had cause for amused reflection...since the date of Simon's birthday was – guess what? – none other than the Thirteenth.

The party was an opulent affair, with exotic foodstuffs provided by outside caterers and a huge array of every kind of drink, including copious amounts of champagne. There was a marquee on the lawn with tables and chairs, and one large room had been cleared and made into a disco, complete with strobe lighting and a wise-cracking DJ. Simon's parents – and even his grandparents – were there, together with older suited family friends, as well as the young set.

Alison immediately stood out as the most exceptional girl at the gathering, appearing almost to glow as if a special spotlight were trained on her. Tall and lithe, with long honey hair and sharp aristocratic features, she wore a low-cut backless black dress which showed acres of beautiful smooth tanned skin. Once, I was standing nearby when she leant forward to reach a tray of canapés and her dress billowed out to give me a tantalizing glimpse of nipple. My heart raced, and I was fired with fugitive dream yearnings and roguish visions of conquest.

She appeared so elegant and superior I thought she'd be unapproachable – certainly by a lowly student such as myself, out of his social depth and underdressed in jeans and a sweatshirt. I expected her to be the girlfriend of some local landowner's son or stockbroker, but continued observation revealed no particular man in tow. Late on in the evening I found Alison dancing with several other girls-in-long-dresses, and with the kind of spontaneity that only too much alcohol can provide, I launched myself into their circle, swinging, shaking and hopping with what I felt to be great aplomb.

Gradually the other girls melted back, leaving me in a one-to-one with Alison. When the music stopped, I waited for her to make an excuse and join her friends, but amazingly she started to chat, asking me whom did I know, and what did I think of the party. Hearing her speak nicely and normally emboldened me, and I suggested we get more drinks and find somewhere quieter. We drifted into the now sparsely populated marquee and sat down in a dark corner. In no time we were kissing ferociously, and when I put a hand inside Alison's dress, she reciprocated with vigour.

Already swimming in alcohol, my mind was pushed further into rarefied realms as I contemplated full congress with this rampant debutante. But how make it happen? *Where* make it happen? In a house swarming with parents and other relatives, trying the bedrooms was inadvisable; and as for the night garden, beyond the canvas, it was illuminated like a football field. And there were other issues fighting for attention as the groping intensified. I didn't have any condoms on me, and trying to borrow some from one of my legless friends would involve an embarrassing fiasco. And overlaying all this was something else still: the inescapable question of arithmetic. Crunch time for the numbers freak had finally arrived.

In my then two and a half years of sexual activity I'd had twelve lovers: two relationships proper, five short-lived casual affairs, and five one-night stands. The last affair had petered out about a month ago, and in that time I'd long contemplated this inevitable moment when – fright of frights! horror of horrors! – I'd have to confront none other than The Thirteenth Girl.

Okay, you can say it's only superstition; but when you have a phobia about something, as I do about this, the tendency is to *make it happen*, albeit unwillingly. Whether thirteen is intrinsically unlucky or not then becomes academic: it may not be unlucky for you, but *it is for me!* I don't pretend to understand the covert workings of the universe – why some people know things are going to happen in advance; why others are accident-prone beyond all reasonable odds – all I have is my experience, and when it comes to the number thirteen that experience is invariable bad.

Normally I deal with the situation by avoidance; for example I never initiate nor truncate an activity at thirteen minutes past the hour, I either move on twelve or wait till fourteen; similarly I would never use a locker numbered thirteen or queue at checkout thirteen at a supermarket. But in the matter of sex, avoidance would entail becoming celibate for the rest of my life when I wasn't even out of my teens! No, there had to be a Thirteenth Girl. If I passed on Alison then she wouldn't be it, the next girl would, and so on. The problem was intractable.

Once again, I considered the hypothetical case of a man

who has a premonition his aeroplane is going to crash, so instead of taking his intended flight he takes a different one – and *that's* the one that crashes. The moral is: whatever he does or doesn't do, he will automatically seek out the doom which awaits him. There is no escape.

So, I returned to my fatalistic starting point, at the same time reflecting that Alison's warm body was ostensibly the furthest thing from doom I could imagine. And then, as if taking my thoughts as her cue, she looked endearingly into my face and said,

'My place is empty. Parents are staying over in London. You want to come back for coffee?'

'My favourite drink,' I said.

Alison's 'place' was even more splendid than Simon's family seat. Lying at the end of a two-hundred-yard private drive, its various wings, annexes, towers and balconies came across with unreal gothic exoticism in the clear moonlight. Alison paid the taxi, and as I watched its red tail lamps retreat, I got a strong sense of the spooky isolation in which the rich live. For a second I felt panicky, fearing that now we were alone Alison might show her true Thirteenth Girl colours and transform into a vampire or a witch.

But this attack of paranoia was quickly dispelled. As soon as we got into her bedroom, passion took over and we sank together into an abyss of pleasure which nothing – not even triskaidekaphobia – could spoil. Far from it; in fact I concluded gleefully that Alison was proving to be my best lover ever. I even considered that perhaps the Curse of Thirteen had finally been lifted.

Alison threw me out at seven in the morning – before the housekeeper had a chance to see me and report back to the parents. I managed to hitch a lift into town, then I phoned Simon, who wasn't pleased to be woken so early and with a hangover. I had taken Alison's number and promised to call and arrange something, but that day we lads got involved in another drunken binge, and the following day – Saturday – we drove back to Bristol to attend another big party there.

6

Over the next week or so I thought deeply about Alison and that rapturous night we'd spent together, wondering if a repeat performance was viable. I'd quizzed Simon, but he knew nothing about her; she was probably a friend of a friend of one of his sisters. I made vague resolutions to invite her up to stay for a weekend, but then whenever I thought of the rich-kid life she'd described to me – riding, tennis, society functions – I seriously doubted we could ever make a pair. Not that that would rule out the purely physical attractions, of course. Twice or three times I was on the point of phoning her, but each time I found an excuse to delay. Perhaps it was residual unlucky feeling about her number which held me back. Anyway, soon afterwards I met another girl – Zandra – who shortly became The Fourteenth Girl, and Alison was pushed into history.

But still I kept thinking about her, fantasizing about her, quite obsessively at times. When I had sex with Zandra I often pretended she was Alison. For a while I entertained the idea of contacting Alison and trying to cultivate a liaison with her alongside Zandra – get Alison up to speed, so to speak, then perhaps change over like in a relay race – but viewed soberly the logistics seemed too complex and a recipe for self-fulfilling disaster.

When Zandra and I finally split, I again gave serious thought to contacting Alison; but nearly six months had passed since the party, and the whole idea was now seeming mildly ludicrous. I would get out the piece of paper which contained her phone number and look at it over and over. I never got up the nerve to ring though – I simply couldn't think of how, from a cold start, to explain myself after half a year of silence. At the very best she'd think it irksome; at worst she could be hostile or not even remember who I was. Again I let the matter lie, considering it best to preserve my illusion of Alison rather than risk exchanging it for an unpalatable reality.

Not long after that, I had three crazy flings in a short period – Girls Sixteen, Seventeen and Eighteen. (Girl Fifteen was a bit on the side during Zandra's reign.) I was on a roll, and the magic number of Twenty was coming within my reach. But however much I saturated myself in female flesh, it was still the contours of *Alison's* body which defined the landscape of my erotic longings.

So, a full year went by, and Simon's birthday came around once again. I was automatically invited to the party, and in one way it seemed perfect for resolving the deadlock over Alison – I could at last find out how things stood. But there was another factor in play which served to excite all my old anxieties. This time Simon's birthday not only fell on the Thirteenth, but on a *Friday* the Thirteenth...

Oh, how I hate Friday the Thirteenths! Even as much as a month in advance I start to feel the fear; just the sight of it on calendars and in diaries is enough to make me nauseous. I conjecture a countdown to some terrible horror, some tragic denouement, each day bringing me closer to the inevitable, the unstoppable, for I nor anyone else is capable of holding up a hand and halting *time*.

But I was determined not to be overwhelmed by the fear. I told myself it was all in my head, and if I backed down I'd regret it forever. There was some comfort to be had from acting strong, though on the drive to Kingston I still suffered considerable twinges of foreboding. I ran through the various potential scenarios once again, soothing myself with strong lager...

What was the worst that could happen? If Alison was annoyed, so be it; but she'd hardly go as far as doing me *harm*, would she? Perhaps she wouldn't even be there, which would be a small relief, but also an anticlimax. But then there was the upside: she could be pleased to see me and not have taken umbrage, accepting what we did as a casual encounter which might now go further. I fancied Alison more crazily than ever, and the prospect of going to bed with her again was stomach-meltingly delicious. I resolved this time I'd do it right and make her mine – thirteen or no thirteen.

And at the party she *was* there! Her sublime image was a velvet sword, running me through with dream emotion. She was wearing that same black dress, displaying the immense flatlands of her long, tanned back, and impressive hill country of cleavage as she turned. When she caught sight of me, she acted a little coy and reddened somewhat – just as you'd expect on the next encounter after a night of demonstrative passion. The effect on me was for the entire year-long interval to seemingly compress into an acceptable span – a week, a few days perhaps – and with that my confidence was restored, and I knew exactly what to do.

'Alison!' I said, coming closer. 'Great to see you. I was so hoping you'd be here. You see, what happened was I *lost* your phone number...And I don't know your surname to look it up, and I don't live locally...Ridiculous! Ha, ha. Anyway, how are you?'

She said she was fine, and although she seemed a little incredulous at my explanation, she wasn't offish. We talked at length about trivial things, then we had a session in the disco, and later we circulated separately for a while. All the time Alison maintained an ambiguous cordiality towards me, which I intuited was a front for her true feelings. Was she interested in having me back to her place again, or was she just being well-mannered and secretly regarded me as an oaf? I would have to wait to find out, and in the meantime I helped myself to liberal amounts of the drink on offer.

When I was sufficiently primed by alcohol, I tested the situation by making a pass at Alison. She didn't flinch, but there was something restrained and mechanical about the way she kissed me – quite unlike her response of a year ago. The warning signs were there, and I should have read them, but I saw only what I wanted to see. Tasting Alison's lips again drove me to such a delirious pitch that I had to have her – I'd do anything. So when she broke away and whispered huskily, 'Shall we go back to my place?' my only thought was how lucky for me everything was turning out.

This time the entrance to Alison's stately pile wasn't locked, nor was the burglar alarm armed. I sensed other people in the house, and when Alison avoided the staircase and led me along a panelled hallway, I started to whiff danger. Feeling I was in a dream which had taken a characteristic detour from normality, I followed Alison into a large parlour where three men in black bow ties and dinner jackets were standing sipping brandy. They were all of equal height – about six feet two – and one of them looked to be in his fifties, while the other two were in their twenties. The older man and one of the younger ones had dark moustaches. All three glared at me with impassive hostility.

Alison said, 'How was the meeting with Lord Winterton?'

'Fine...fine,' said the older man, obviously her father. 'We ironed out the few quibbles he had, and now the deal's going ahead...' He gestured towards me. 'Is this *him*?'

'Yes, this is him,' Alison said.

'Was luring him here easy?'

'He took the bait like a pony gobbling sugar.'

I tried to speak, but my throat had become constricted. In addition, my hands were trembling and felt light and flyaway as though they were filled with gas. I croaked and eventually got my words out. 'W-What's all this about...?'

Alison turned to face me and said, eyes ablaze, 'Wouldn't you like to know!' Then she said, 'Okay,' to one of the brothers, who in turn called though a set of open double doors.

I couldn't make out what I was seeing at first – the meaning of it, that is...A bent-up and gnarled old lady, who looked like a refugee from some nineteenth century novel, came forward with a baby's carry-cot and laid it on the table in front of us. Alison said, 'Thank you, Nanny,' and Nanny retired.

Staring down at the little pink sleeping head with its sparse gossamer covering, I felt no sense of paternal pride or similar emotion, only a detached acceptance that the child was mine, and a terrifying clarity at coming face to face with fundamentals. Of course...this was what sex is *for* – not for pleasure, not for kicks, not for inflating the ego; although it does all those things to encourage us to partake; but its real purpose now stood nakedly revealed – baby-making, reproduction of the species, the continuation of the thread of life down through the generations, evolution by whatever means, at whatever cost...

'You bastard!' I heard Alison saying through my reverie. 'You take me to bed – and then what? Not a word. Not a phone call. Not a Christmas card. Nothing in a whole year. *Nothing! Nothing! Nothing!* And then you come along – with a *pathetic lie* about losing my phone number – and expect a repeat performance...Just like that!'

Our child woke up and began to cry. Nanny appeared from the shadows and took it away to give succour.

'Why didn't you have an abortion?' I blurted out, immediately regretting the words as my gaze alighted on a small framed picture of the Virgin Mary on the dresser.

'Abortion is a sin against Almighty God,' said the moustachioed brother as all three men edged closer, menace on their faces.

Oh shit...I mentally intoned as the horror heightened and the greater truth about my predicament fully obtruded. I hadn't been brought here *just* to look at a baby: they meant to *do* something to me. *What...?* A beating up? *Worse* than a beating up? Images of torture and mutilation zapped through my mind like a fast-forwarding music video directed by Hieronymus Bosch. The brothers were taking off their jackets, removing their cufflinks and ties...These people weren't just rich nutters, they were *religious* rich nutters – obsessive, maybe even a touch psycho...Was it time to panic yet? My heart raced so furiously it was like it had spawned an ensemble of subsidiary hearts throughout my torso, neck and skull, all throbbing in a dreadful percussive sync...

Sleeves were being rolled...When I noticed a rack of kitchen knives on the far wall, I finally did panic and made a wild rush for the door; but the two hefty brothers pounced and grabbed an arm each, twisting them behind my back. Trust Alison to have a pair of siblings like these – but then she would, wouldn't she? Having now totally trapped my arms, they each hooked a foot around my two respective ankles, anchoring my legs firmly to the floor. I tried to wriggle, but they bent my arms back further, making me gasp at the pain.

Whatever it was that was coming, I would just have to take it...This thought seemed slow and stretched-out like mozzarella cheese; and then everything – reality itself – seemed similarly slowed and stretched. Alison was taking an inordinately long time to reach me from a distance of only six or seven feet, and I was seeing her so clearly – her fine bone structure, nicely muscled bare shoulders beyond the straps of the dress, beautiful supermodel legs revealed now as she swished open the slit in its skirt...

The bare knee rising free of the black fabric was exquisitely sexual, and contrasted fascinatingly with the primal hatred in her eyes and snarling animal mouth as she at last truly resembled what she was: The Thirteenth Girl! a creature of otherworldly malevolence, a doom-carrying succubus sent to slay me from the beyond. I closed my thighs as best I could, but unfortunately all I achieved was to further present my genitals rather than protect them. In the nanosecond before she struck, I felt I loved her more than ever...

And then...the pain. I roared as it exploded out of me seemingly to fill the universe and grind time to a ghastly halt, nullifying any possibility of escape, of improvement. This had to be worse than death – worse than anything! But it was all inevitable, my mind was telling me through the agony. If against your better judgement you seek out The Thirteenth Girl on Friday the Thirteenth, what the hell do you expect? I was so overwhelmed I didn't notice at first that Alison now had one of the large carving knives in her grasp and was unzipping my fly...

I struggled hard as she found my member, the voice in my head going crazy, throwing words at me like a succession of high-speed bowling balls: *If you thought being kneed in the nuts was worse than anything, how are you going to rate this?* And at the same time, I was aware of Alison's father rushing up behind her in slow motion and shouting, 'Steady Alison! We've put the frighteners on him enough now...' Then: *'Stop her, for God's sake!'* as the brothers released me and dived for

12

Alison, all four of them massing into a scrummage on the marble tiled floor.

The oddest thing was seeing that part of me which, all of my life, I'd been accustomed to viewing at a fixed distance, now suddenly retreat away, as though on a long spring perhaps. I had kind of tunnel vision, and my manhood was at the end of the tunnel, a long dark rotating tunnel. Before I passed out, I remember Alison looking at me, her face sprayed with a diagonal slash of dripping red, the red covering one breast and soaking into the fabric of the dress; her expression was gentle now, and seemed to be saying: 'I'm sorry...'

I suppose I was lucky really. The cut was a clean one, and the consultant surgeon said that restoring my organ had not been the most difficult of tasks – though a first for him and his team, and good practice should this sort of thing become endemic. The attitude of the doctors and nurses was very light-hearted and jokey like that, once the crisis was over; especially so, the more of a celebrity patient I became.

The press and media interest in the debacle was gigantic, and several of the tabloids picked up on the fact it had happened on Friday the Thirteenth, incorporating this into four-inch-high headlines. I told one reporter who visited me, pretending to be an uncle, that Alison was The Thirteenth Girl, and this too was rapturously taken aboard – one magazine even featured a macabre illustration of a big number thirteen coated with blood, and a mean-looking girl holding a bloody knife with a badge saying No.13 on her collar. It was weird having my most secret hang-ups made manifest and projected hugely onto the screen of mass public interest – a kind of strange enlightenment really.

When I'd recovered, I found myself on *Good Morning*, trying to explain it all to Richard and Judy. They loved the bit about the phobia coming true; but what they found hard to understand was why Alison and I had now decided to get married. I couldn't think up a good answer to that one, and became bashful and tongue-tied, burbling some nonsense about 'fatal attraction' and thinking that several million viewers must now regard me as extremely obtuse. Fortunately, there was a psychologist interviewee on hand to provide the professional angle, and he came in at this point.

He said that one of the best ways of dealing with a phobia is to embrace the feared object or situation in order to desensitise oneself to the triggering effect brought on by association. Clearly that's what I was doing here, he reckoned, and under the numbing glare of the studio lights I was happy to nod my head and agree.

At the trial Alison said she hadn't really meant to do the deed; she'd just got carried away and couldn't stop herself. Her defence of temporary insanity was accepted, and she received a suspended sentence together with an order for outpatient psychiatric treatment. The wedding was the day after – on the Thirteenth, appropriately enough – but by then so much had happened so quickly I was past caring.

With the money Alison got from her family and the money I made from my TV appearances and selling my story worldwide, we moved into a large riverside mansion with a full-time nanny (not the old relic) to look after Bobby, our son. We have a great life now; we don't have to do real work, and as a couple of some fame our list of social engagements is envious.

That psychologist had something, I think. Now I've embraced my phobic object I can't seem to go wrong. When I look at Alison in her specially commissioned 13th Girl tee-shirt, swinging little Bobby up and down through the air and cooing with maternal joy, I know this is how it had to be; my life couldn't have worked out any differently.

So...why worry about it?

THE RUNNER

Rafe evaluated himself in the bathroom mirror as he applied suntan cream to his face, ears and neck for protection during his evening jog...Chunky, swarthy, the usual sullen hangdog expression. He was an ageing, unlovely human being, and there was no pretending otherwise.

Life was too cluttered with precautionary activity, he decided upon finishing the job. Sun cream was necessary to avoid melanomas. As sunglasses were necessary to avoid cataracts. And condoms were necessary to avoid HIV, gonorrhoea, herpes, Hepatitis C and who knows what other nasty diseases as yet undiscovered?

Cigarettes gave you lung cancer, emphysema and hardened arteries. Butter and cheese clogged your arteries with cholesterol. Alcohol weakened your liver, brain...and your arteries. Beefburgers gave you Creutzfeld-Jakob's Disease. Aluminium foil gave you Alzheimer's. Cling film lowered your sperm count.

So much to avoid, cut down on or give up.

He took the path across the golf course, shuffling gradually into his stride and hoping he didn't appear too pathetic to the eyes of onlookers. Being cautious, he didn't want to push himself too much in the early stages and burn out. He knew he should jog at least twice a week to keep up the momentum of his fitness, but he'd been slacking lately; he hadn't done any for nearly three weeks and already he could feel the deficit.

The road loomed ahead and Rafe was glad of the excuse to slow to a halt and let the traffic pass so he could cross. Turning, he glimpsed his reflection full length in the glass walls of the golf course office. His shorts looked too big on him, like those of an old-time heavyweight boxer or

15

footballer. In profile he resembled Alfred Hitchcock in shorts! He felt silly – and conspicuously so. Was there really any point at all to this striving for betterness?

Rafe passed through the stone gateway of the park, onto the parched hay-like grass and commenced the earnest phase of his jog. After five or six hundred yards he was struggling again, his legs as heavy as cast-iron drainpipes, his viscera wound into a Möbius strip of discomfort. Unable to muster the inspiration to force himself onward, he broke into a walk, panting. He felt the full ignominy of being a jogger who can't keep going – an object of ridicule and scorn.

He let five minutes pass then tried again, setting himself a really easy pace, as slow as was possible and still, technically, be considered running. But things kept putting him off. A terrier yapping incessantly to his left; some kids on skateboards trundling along the path; a slight crosswind cooling his cheek. This flotsam of perception was like obstacles thrown in his path, impedances to his already fragile performance. He knew he couldn't keep it up. The next two hundred yards, the next thirty years of life, were impossible.

He sighted the botanical gardens and stopped to open the gates and go inside, as if that had been his intention all along. Regaining his breath among the ginkgoes, silver limes and giant yuccas, he considered how much harder it was to break the pain barrier these days. The simple fact was Rafe just wasn't a natural athlete, and no amount of 'training' would turn him into one. He jogged because he knew it was good for the heart and the metabolism generally; he'd be even heavier if he didn't do it, as he could not diet. But he seldom enjoyed it. He wanted it to be a pleasure but it wasn't.

Rafe's chest – specifically his heart area – ached. Perhaps he was doing himself more harm than good. Jogging in middle age sometimes precipitates a heart attack, he knew. A fatty deposit on the inside of a blood vessel breaks free during the exertion and lodges in one of the arteries feeding the heart. Bingo! He considered himself a suitable subject for just such a misfortune.

Rafe carried on through the gardens and up to the griffin-headed gateposts on the far boundary of the park. He was thinking he'd make another attempt at jogging in ten minutes or so; he simply needed more time to warm up and raise himself to the pitch necessary to make it viable.

Exiting through the gates and coming back onto the road dividing park from golf course, he experienced a wave of un-explained free-floating joy...and then he saw her, in the distance, heading his way at a terrific pace.

Yes, it was definitely her – *that* girl. Rafe had wondered when he was next going to see her – he hadn't seen her in months – and now here she was, about to briefly touch his life once again.

Titian could have painted her as she bounded vigorously along the sweep of the road, wrapped in bronze summer evening sunlight, the half-moon above the treetops behind her as feint as a fingerprint. She didn't jog, she *ran*, taking great long strides, every muscle tensioned to perfect pitch, her sharp straight nose streamlining her passage as her mane of flame wavy hair swelled behind her like a cape.

She wore runner's kit: vest and dinky little shorts in shiny electric blue polyester, trimmed in white. Rafe eyed her with a kind of lust, but it was a lust which went beyond mere car-nality, it was a lust of pure human aesthetics. He drank her in, from the firm pads of her deltoids to the S curves of her biceps and triceps, the taut slabs of her hamstrings, the sen-suous bulges of her calves, the concave stomach and visible ribs, the breasts elevated to pertness by strong pectorals, the buttocks tight and neat, almost like a boy's – but not quite!

Her musculature was beautifully developed, yet she was still lithe and spare and gave the impression of feminine del-icacy. There was nothing hefty about her, nothing of the body builder. She was a perfectly strung and tuned instru-ment: a customised running machine.

She was everything Rafe could never be...and never have.

He'd been glimpsing her sporadically for years now, every

occasion striking a special chord, so that progressively she'd become an icon of his inner life.

Often he saw he fleetingly while driving. She covered immense distances, and her long-striding form could be spotted out along the city's feeder roads and further afield on the dual carriageways, and in and around the satellite villages. Rafe at the wheel would strain his head around for a better view, risking accidents, or rock it from side to side to get that extra sight of her, tiny in his rear-view mirror.

Once, spectacularly, he'd seen her from the window of a train as it rattled across the viaduct and she dodged skilfully around the one-way traffic system below. And unexpectedly on dark winter evenings he'd witness the signature of her wild red hair sketched briefly by his headlights as she pounded through puddles, Cat Woman-like in close-fitting tracksuit and gloves.

He wouldn't want to know her name, where and how she lived, whether or not she was married or cohabiting with a guy or whatever. He wouldn't even want to hear her voice, her views on politics or TV programmes or the state of the country. Anything which would make her more three dimensional would make her less magical.

And as Rafe remained pleasingly ignorant of any other life she might have, he imagined her running perpetually, doing nothing else but running. He thought of her now as if on a never-ending circuit taking in the parks and golf courses of the city, continuing on to the footpaths and bridleways encircling its outlying farms, then over its monument-encrusted hills and far away. And always she would be maintaining her splendid pace, her beautiful lungs filling and emptying tirelessly, her healthy heart making her veins and arteries glow like some neon map of the London Underground. She would never be found flagging, never shuffling, and above all never *walking*!

She could traverse the yellow brick roads of fantasyland, leading him Pied Piper-fashion, and he would follow wherever she chose to go, down through the dark velvet valleys and up onto the diamond-topped peaks. She could cut a swathe through the secret forests of his dreams, where clocks were frozen midway between night and dawn, and every configuration of leaf and branch formed coded signposts. She could circumnavigate the globe, tracing great circles as she treaded down the undulating continents and skimmed lightly over the shimmering oceans. She could use the planets as stepping stones and bounce right out of the Solar System in her air-cushioned Reeboks and be gone forever...or perhaps she'd return periodically like a comet, always welcome, always remarkable, always out of reach.

NORTH

When I was a child I used to have incredible dreams of escape, where I would transcend my ordinary surroundings and head North, always North, into landscapes of successively increasing phantasmagorical beauty...fields of waist-high silky grass, blown by the breeze into whorls, eddies and lazy zigzags of impossible sensuousness...endless flat deserts where hugely distant minareted cities sparkled under phosphorescent pink skies...dawn-silhouetted mountain ranges, high as the highest clouds, clothed in a fur of deep green forest and studded with golden temples...

It wasn't just the visual appeal of these scenes which enchanted me, it was the sense of complete liberation and happiness which accompanied my journeys there. To my child's mind it seemed obvious this should be the goal of life – the pursuance and greater discovery of such places, or states, depending on how one regarded them.

But having decided this I soon hit a snag. These special dreams couldn't be conjured at will, and the more I yearned for them the more elusive they became, the more ephemeral their pleasures. Often, I would realise within the dream that I was dreaming, and this would wake me before I fully attained the magic dimension. In compensation, I tried to equate the real geography of my neighbourhood with that of my dream world, thinking that if I headed North far enough and purposefully enough then reality would turn into a dream. On Sunday walks with Dad out into the country, I fantasised this would happen.

It was this kind of thinking, I suppose, which lay behind my attempt to run away from home.

On the night in question Mum and Dad were rowing again. I tiptoed out of my bedroom, down the stairs and hung on the banister, listening. His voice rose up to big crescendos, then fell away like waves crashing on the shore; whilst hers was whiny and pleading. He was threatening to leave again – he always did when things came to a head – and this time it sounded more serious than usual. I got this intense feeling of fear in the pit of my stomach as though I'd been sucked into an infinite tunnel and could never find my way back.

I returned to my bed, but just couldn't quieten down. I waited and waited for sleep, counting the moments on some giant mental abacus. Eventually I heard Mum and Dad ascend the stairs to bed, their conflagration now burnt down to the odd few grunts and grumbles. When the noise of Dad's rhythmic snoring was established, I took that as my cue. I got up, dressed and slipped out of the back door, silent as a wraith.

The night was dark and velvety as I headed off out of our cul-de-sac and turned North, naturally, towards the country. As I progressed, a feeling of wonder and escapism filled up every space in my body like a transfusion of some new special high-octane blood. I knew what I was doing was technically wrong, but I felt that someone somewhere must understand me, and that made it all right.

A car went past, its quotidian nature reminding me ominously that this adventure wasn't actually a dream, that real cause and effect still obtained. Still, it did have a distinctly dreamlike feel. The silent petrified quality of the roadside trees and the rugby goalposts in the playing fields opposite was pleasing; and the sombre shapes of the railway bridge and the chocolate factory looked magical against the indigo sky. It wasn't hard to *imagine* this was a dream.

I got down as far as the electricity sub-station before a passing police car noticed me and picked me up. I thought Mum and Dad would be furious, but the shock of what had happened coupled with the presence of uniforms in our front room neutralised any anger.

Weeks later, unable to resolve the issue of why I'd run away, they took me to a child psychiatrist, who would get to the bottom of things, they said. He kept asking me what made me do it, probing and coaxing like it was some riddle to which I was expected to guess the answer. All I could tell him was that I was trying to make my dreams become real – and who wouldn't want to do that?

Now I often think of my childhood dreams and that runaway attempt as I patrol the endless supermarket aisles of my psyche, shopping for a meaning to it all. I was, however briefly, completely happy when in the grip of those events, and I've been far from happy since. I am not happy now.

Dad *did* leave eventually, going to live with a secretary from his work. After a period of intermittent contact, he broke away altogether; I haven't seen nor spoken to him in over four years. And Mum has now passed on. A year ago, she started to get terrible pains in her stomach, which turned out to be cancer. She had an operation, but it wasn't a success and poor Mum just faded away.

So, I live in the house on my own now, and the emptiness of it frightens me sometimes. When I finish work in the evenings I tend to hang around in bars or go to the cinema – anything to delay the dread moment of going back and having my loneliness swamp me like a heavy black blanket.

Work itself is not going at all well. There's an unshakeable bad atmosphere between my supervisor and myself; he's constantly looking for and finding fault, and never acknowledges anything positive I achieve. In truth I do keep making mistakes, and I just can't concentrate for any length of time. I'm constantly watching myself going through the motions and see no point to any of it – I don't understand how the others tolerate work so cheerfully. Work seems to me like a great Möbius strip of nonsensicalness, perpetuated for ever.

I just couldn't face it this morning so I phoned in sick. Being at home on a weekday reminds me of sickness as a child, being looked after by Mum, getting my boiled egg and soldiers in bed and then coming downstairs to an open fire to watch schools TV in my dressing gown. What unalloyed bliss!

I don't think I'll go back to work – not ever. The thought

both comforts and frightens me, and that familiar sense of confusion descends. I feel as though I've been hollowed out and the space inside me filled with some lighter-than-air gas. I wonder how to pass the time, and suddenly any of the tasks I could perform – grocery shopping, doing the washing-up or vacuuming, writing out cheques to pay bills – seem gargantuan and utterly beyond my capabilities.

What is happening to me? Some kind of metamorphosis, I reckon. But into what?

I spend the rest of the day staring at the wallpaper, projecting all manner of extraneous patterns, faces and whatever into its texture. I keep drifting off and coming back, a balloon lightly tethered on a long string. I try to think happy thoughts and not scare myself with heavy ones.

Towards evening I decide to take a walk, savouring the magic as the sky darkens to Prussian blue and the first few stars appear, and lights come on. I head North, of course, past the playing fields and the chocolate factory; and I remember with a smile my runaway attempt as a child and connect with that feeling.

Then in a giant rush of joy, revelation dawns. All this time I've been accepting the straitjacket limitations of 'reality' when there never was any need – my dream world has always been there for me, accessible, but I just couldn't see it. The key to everything, the thing I've just realised, is that there is no difference! Dream is reality; reality is dream.

The first thing I do is take off all my clothes. The exhilaration, the freedom I feel is unmatched since early childhood. It doesn't matter if people see me because they're just part of my dream – everything is!

Now I'm really getting somewhere!

The next stage in my enlightenment is the realisation that I can control things by *thought* – mind is all! I think I'm walking along a pavement, therefore I am; but if I think I can *sink* into it as though it's quicksand, then that too is equally possible. I experiment, my feet and calves disappearing into the flagstones up to the knees, then re-emerging. Mmmnn...interesting...

But why go down when you can go U-UPPPPP!!!

I think *fly* and start to make pedalling motions, which lift me into the air in a gentle circular path as though on a fairground big wheel...

'*Whey! hey! hey!*' I say as I get to twenty feet, thirty feet. The neighbourhood below me is starting to look quaint and idealised like a Bavarian village, the buildings and people reduced to mere schemata, a pleasing backdrop to accompany my travels.

I get higher, very high, and then start to accelerate, becoming more purposefully aligned like a bullet to its target.

I zoom out across the wide landscape, over the hump-backed bridges of childhood fairyland, through vast deserts strewn with the debris of decayed civilizations, up wooded escarpments of impossible height, past palaces made of mirrors built in the clouds, and all the time there's a great booming in my ears like a drum beat in the form of a voice which speaks faster and faster the words all congealing together into a rat tat tat of pure significance as I go faster than sound faster than light all the way along that route leading North and this time I know I'm never coming back and I'm finally going to find out what lies at the end of it.

CAUGHT IN THE LABYRINTH

Janine Bailey had reached a point: sometime this evening, as near as could be calculated, she would be thirty-three-point three recurring years of age. She had occupied the planet for exactly one third of a century. It was certainly something to think about. In a kind of birthday celebration, she drank a glass of chilled Chablis, poured from a half bottle, to accompany her dinner-for-one of poached salmon, mange tout and new potatoes. But she hardly felt in the mood for festivities.

Earlier in the day Janine had recognised that her recent most pressing problem – Geoff Hills chasing her – had at last become major. It simply wasn't going to fade away of its own accord as she'd hoped, but would worsen inexorably till she herself took decisive action. She drank more wine, but it wasn't helping to dissipate the tension. At this precise point in time, she could do nothing about stopping Geoff Hills, nor could she cure the unnerving sense of stage-fright which had developed since it all began; so in order to do something to give shape to the chaos of thoughts filling her head, she invented a pseudo-problem to work on: Trace the *exact* moment she first became positively aware of his intentions.

Janine remembered well the time she'd looked up from her lunch in the works canteen to discover Hills staring directly at her. He didn't look away immediately the way most men would but continued to gaze meaningfully in the attempt to make a point of his interest...Or was she now colouring the occasion with hindsight? She had to separate her original impressions from later embellishments. What had she thought *at the time*? Probably very little. Men stared at her frequently – it was a fact of life.

But with Hills it didn't stop at staring. Every day he saw her he would say ebulliently, 'Hello Janine. How are you today?' and when their paths crossed subsequently, he would say, 'Hello again,' or, 'We can't go on meeting like this.' His exaggerated smiles and winks, his cloying conviviality were far above and beyond the call of mere politeness to a work colleague. He'd go out of his way to initiate small talk then follow up its content on future occasions, giving it importance and meaning it didn't deserve. He had the knack of showing up as if by magic at strategic times and places, such as the canteen at 12.45 when Janine generally went to lunch, or the car park at 5.25 when she generally went home. While all this was going on Janine was asking herself *Is this behaviour natural?* knowing the very fact she was asking meant it wasn't. But she gave Hills the benefit of the doubt on the grounds that he could just be an over-friendly sort of person – it didn't necessarily mean he *fancied* her.

Yet at some level she felt herself to be the object of Hills's fancy. She was always unnaturally nervous and self-conscious in his company. When he confronted her, she was caught off-balance and couldn't be herself, resorting to returning his pleasantries in an act which was the perfect mirror of Hills's own. In this she was capitulating to Hills's version and at the same time giving him the wrong signals. She wanted to stem the tide but couldn't, for Hills had a weirdly hypnotic effect on her. When he was doing his routines she entered a transfixed state, viewing him with strange detachment as though he were a painting and not real life, and becoming acutely – almost painfully – aware of all the tiny ambient details of his persona.

Everything about him came over as phoney. The artificial showbiz patter laced with jokes and wisecracks...The TV quizmaster's fixed smile and glistening manic eyes...The constant sense of innuendo he created, implying that he and Janine were already involved, part of a grand conspiracy, two of a kind who talked the same language, who were made for each other. Janine felt no reciprocation for these sentiments. The idea of Hills as an amorous partner was absurd and vaguely revolting. What she saw before her was a man of nearly forty trying his hardest to act ten years younger. A man with no dress sense: his dowdy single-breasted suits, small collars and thin ties were out of date and uninspired. A man in dubious physical shape: his stomach bulged behind his shirt front, he had a double chin and the beginnings of jowls. A man who wore his hair too long and had *sideboards*. Very Seventies. Janine could detect no redeeming features in Hills; all she saw were the negatives – the yellow teeth and cigarette breath, the imprecisely shaved stubble around the base of his nose punctuating the broken capillaries, the ugly sheaf of wild black hair sprouting inside one ear. This man was about the furthest thing from a desirable, eligible male that Janine could imagine. The fact he had attached himself to her, limpet-like, was a source of unending enigma and turmoil, the combination producing a kind of hopeless bafflement.

Throughout Janine had tried to see it from Hills's point of view. What exactly did he think would *happen* if and when this 'relationship' got off the ground? Was it just a casual affair to him, a quick fling, one of a multitude of conquests to add to his many-splendid sexual portfolio? Or – shock! horror! – was it *love*, the real thing; were his intentions, as they say, honourable? Janine conjectured an extended courtship with Geoff Hills, a gradual merging of their separateness into a unity, culminating in a vision of herself decked in white lace with Hills beside her in a dove grey morning coat, an expression of beatific adoration on his face...*Yuk! Yuk! No thanks...*

But she was getting way ahead of herself and had yet to address the prime purpose of this discovery. When was the moment she first became aware...? She scanned the various incidents, this time in strict chronological order, and came up with as close to the answer as she was going to get. It had to be around the time Hills first sat with her for lunch. The strangeness of a salesman going out of his way to sit with a group of secretaries was felt not only by herself but also by several others on the table who exchanged mildly amused glances. Of course, people from different departments did intermingle at lunch, but it was always the same people according to established convention. If strangers did show up at a table it was usually 'by invitation'. Who sat with whom at lunch was as rigidly codified as a military tattoo. So when Hills's plate of steak and chips appeared next to Janine Bailey's cottage cheese salad that was the danger signal. Up till then his behaviour hadn't really struck her as important; afterwards she felt somehow implicated by it – that was the key: her own sense of implication. This was not hindsight, Janine reflected. It was there and then that Hills's agenda was manifest. Yes, that was the moment, it had to be...

Janine finished her meal and her wine. The momentary consolation of the pseudo-problem was over, and now she would have to spend the rest of the evening till she went to bed, and no doubt beyond that, pondering the real problem and its latest critical development. For earlier on this very day – Janine Bailey's thirty-third and a third birthday – Geoff Hills had stalked her to her car and actually asked the fatal question.

'...How would you like to go out to dinner with me – perhaps tomorrow, or even tonight if you like.'

'I'd love to...' Janine had said. *Why had she said that?* – a total lie; an unintentional lie brought on by the knee-jerk nervousness that Hills induced in her. 'It's a bit difficult at the moment,' she went on, desperately improvising. 'My mother's staying with me...' This time an intentional lie – the best she could come up with under pressure.

'Okay then, some other time. How long is the old girl going to be around?'

'Oh...a week at least, perhaps longer. You know what mothers are like.' Janine found herself fixating on the brass reinforced corners of Hills's briefcase.

'Right. We'll set a date as soon as she's gone. Looking forward to it.'

Smiling, Hills wheeled around and headed for his own car, leaving Janine Bailey to flounder in a sea of self-reproach, wondering *What went wrong? Why did it go wrong? Why does it always go wrong...?*

Poor Janine Bailey.

*   *   *   *

28

Over the following days Janine's dread of bumping into Hills grew to phobic proportions. She felt like an escaped prisoner of war constantly on the lookout for the Gestapo. Never before had the communal areas of the workplace seemed so fraught with impending menace. Inside her office she was well insulated and felt reasonably safe, but as soon as she set foot outside the fear started. She was aware the fear was disproportionate to the actual threat; it was becoming fear of its own making, and that fact added to her overall sense of insecurity.

At bottom she felt she'd handled the Hills situation really badly. All she'd needed to have done when he asked her out was said, 'No Geoff, I'm sorry, I can't. You see, I'm involved with someone.' That would have put a stop to him for sure. And if by chance he did try his luck again she could have referred him to this original 'no', strengthening and consolidating it till Hills got the message once and for all. Now when Hills tried again, as was inevitable, it would be almost impossible to refuse on these terms having provisionally accepted before. If only she'd seen all this coming and *prepared* a refusal in advance. She'd thought about the situation long enough, but none of that thinking was constructive. She was a fool — that was her basic problem. She just couldn't see the right path of action based on the dictates of self-interest.

But as the week drew to a close, Janine's mood improved. Being a salesman, Hills was often out of the building, and Janine had taken to scanning the car park for his gunmetal company Sierra. If it was absent then so was he — and if it was absent on a *Friday afternoon* then she could be reasonably certain she was rid of him till Monday at the earliest. Fridays were nearly always good days. 'Thank God it's Friday' or 'TGIF' was what everyone said, and it was so true. Janine had a responsible job which she liked, but the Friday panacea applied to her as much as to the deadheads on the production line or the gargoyles in dispatch.

Janine Bailey was the managing director's personal assistant. As such she had the distinction of being the most exalted member of the secretarial staff in the building. Some

29

people thought she was stuck-up, which was a pity because in truth that wasn't the case. But she couldn't deny that her image probably contributed to this impression. Tall and stately, with chin held high as she walked, her clothes and make-up of fashion model status, her straight ash-blonde hair styled in a long geometrically precise bob, she cut a very superior figure. But looking this good was an essential part of her job, and if the girls in the typing pool said things behind her back, Janine contented herself with the knowledge her salary was three times theirs.

The Friday euphoria continued on into the evening when Janine went out to eat with her friend Abigail, afterwards dropping in at a wine bar. Determined to keep up the atmosphere, Janine ordered a bottle of champagne. She was doing most of the talking tonight, the chief subject being Hills. Alcohol aided her loquacity, and soon she'd told near enough the whole story, feeling flooded with relief having unburdened herself of the stress.

'Why don't you just tell him to get stuffed?' Abigail said. 'I would.'

'I know you would,' said Janine.

'His ego will be a little bruised, but by next week he'll be chasing someone else. If you *don't* burst his bubble, he'll go on thinking *you* fancy *him*.'

'I know...I know...'

'You aren't having a lot of luck with men lately, are you? How long has it been since you split up with David?'

'A year...'

'A year? – as long as that? And you haven't been out with anyone in that time?'

'No.'

'You're out of practice, kid. You need to brush up on your basic training.'

'I'm not sure I ever had my basic training,' Janine admitted.

By Saturday evening Janine's euphoria had all but drained to the last drop. She spent the morning food shopping and, in the afternoon, bought herself a high-necked white blouse and two pairs of shoes. After her late coffee with Abigail, she knew that from now until Monday she would not have meaningful contact with another human being. Abigail was going out with her latest boyfriend; she would sleep with him tonight and spend the majority of Sunday under the duvet. Janine would get the details next week – but the details of Abigail's sex life were always the same, always drearily positive. Abigail was the only local friend of Janine's with whom she had sufficient rapport to go out with on a one-to-one basis. There were *couples* of course, usually home-bound due to young children, whom she could drop in to see. But generally she found this a drag; intruding into their closely meshed domestic scenarios tended to emphasise her own aloneness. If she were a man she could hang about in bars, but as a single woman she'd just be molested. She spent ten minutes trying to decide whether or not to queue for the cinema and decided against it. There was no alternative but to go home, watch television and read.

So, the pattern of Janine Bailey's week had come nearly full cycle. All that was left was the final descent into yet another claustrophobic Sunday, and the whole thing would begin again. She had huge endless prairies of time to herself now. Before she split up with her husband, she reckoned this was what she needed – time to be alone, time to be free of the constraints of duty, time to dream, time to plan an autonomous future. But now she actually had the time it was oppressive, crying out to be filled, making her work to find things to do so she wouldn't end up just staring at the walls. Time before the separation had one quality, time now another; but neither had the quality which she sought. If only she could get together with *the right man*...

When she was an adolescent girl, ignorant of the ways of relationships, she thought that once she met this right man everything would change and magically fall into place. Now at thirty-three, after several relationships including an eight-year marriage, she still basically retained the same frame of mind – was still waiting for *him*. Only now she could no longer pretend the wait had any real validity. She could imagine herself in the same position at sixty-three, or ninety-three.

And if she were to get involved with another man, she would again crave freedom knowing that if she had it, she wouldn't want it! There was no answer. It was all a pointless labyrinth which you wandered around in, looking for ways out, constantly bumping your head on its low ceilings, only to end up in the same place, forced to repeat the same steps over and over, the whole process becoming more and more nightmarish with each iteration.

On Monday morning Janine felt an extra edge of agitation as she breakfasted and got herself ready for work. Thoughts of Hills filled her mind. She was angry with him for the trouble he'd caused her and the trouble he would cause in the future – the *near* future. As a result of her anger, she was slowing herself down and not checking everything was turned off properly. Concentrate and calm yourself, she mentally intoned. She mustn't be late – not today.

Rushing downstairs, she stopped abruptly and was drawn back into the bedroom to say one last goodbye to Boris, her teddy bear. She gave him another kiss, patted him on the head and said sorry that she had to leave him at a time like this. As she retreated with a final wave, she had the idea he was angry with her. Then she looked at her watch – *quarter to nine!* – and dashed back down, not daring to consider the oven or toaster again. She slipped on her flat driving shoes (her high heels were in the car), picked up her bag and was out of the front door too soon, so it seemed. She would be late – a least seven or eight minutes, perhaps ten.

After an outrageous piece of overtaking which gained her virtually no advantage, Janine settled into the slow stream of traffic. Her thoughts returned to Boris and how she had considered his 'feelings' relative to herself. With a smile she remembered the cartoon about the man who fell in love with an inflatable doll – a comic hyperbole which worked because it contained a general truth about the way people project their emotions onto others and onto things. Janine had a penchant for quirks like that. There was the germ of an idea here which she might try to develop into a piece of writing. She would think about it through the day, and in the evening would get

32

something down on paper. Already the prospect had caused an uplift of her spirits.

No one saw Janine Bailey slip into her office at nine minutes past nine. She knew her boss wouldn't yet be in the adjoining office because his BMW 535 wasn't in its space. Hills's Sierra was evident, however. He was obviously making an early start to the week.

The morning went smoothly. At the appointed hour, three businessmen from Frankfurt arrived to have talks with Janine's boss, and Janine handed out the paperwork, took notes and kept them supplied with coffee. When one o'clock arrived the leader of the delegation, a suave man in his fifties who insisted on being called Kurt, made a point of inviting Janine to join the group for lunch. This happened quite often, and it was here that Janine came into her own. She had a highly important function to perform, which was to be the rose set among the thorns of business dealing. Apart from being good to look at, her conversation was encyclopaedic, and she could enliven any discussion with complete aplomb.

The party lunched at the Maltravers Hotel, the usually company entertainment spot, a mere hundred yards from the premises. Afterwards they retired to the lounge for further drinking and talk. Janine was waiting for a tray of drinks at the bar when she was startled by a movement to her left and turned sharply. There standing right up close and grinning at her was Geoff Hills.

'Hello, Beautiful. How's your mum?'

'...She's fine,' Janine said. Already her body was starting to go rigid with tension. It was a reflex action she couldn't control.

'Still staying with you, is she?'

'Yes...for a while longer. She doesn't want to go home and be on her own, you see.'

Hills took a slurp of his lager and a puff of his cigarette. 'She's on her own in the day when you're here. That must be a bit boring for the old girl.'

'Oh, she gets out and about, goes shopping visits museums, that kind of thing...' Janine felt exasperated. There was nothing she could do except continue the pretence.

'Perhaps she might give you a night off...?'

'Um...she'd get upset if she didn't see me *all* day...' Janine could feel herself going red. 'It's best to wait, I think.'

Hills was grinning with sardonic triumph. He obviously *knew* she was stalling him and was acting along in a kind of double bluff, irony at her expense. Janine was cornered: she couldn't say yes and she couldn't say no. So, like an idiot she kept saying *mañana*.

'How about a drink now?' Hills said.

'No, it's alright, I've got one coming. I'm with my boss and some other people.'

'You're with the Germans, I know. Go on, they can wait. Have a quick one on me...'

'If it'll make you happy...'

At this moment Janine's tray arrived.

'Too late,' she said, picking it up and walking away with it, being extra careful not to spill any as her hands were shaking.

Teddy was looking a little forlorn and despondent when I said goodbye to him this morning. I closed my front door with a pang of guilt, realizing I hadn't given him his full ration of love and affection.

Janine read back the two sentences and tried to decide where to go from here. She wanted to develop the theme and avoid the trap of autobiography, but she needed to flesh out her narrator and build up some momentum. So, she got the narrator to continue talking about her day with the occasional back reference to Teddy whenever a moment of anxiety arose. Hills was called 'the nasty man'. *I wished Teddy was here to give me comfort now that I'd come upon the nasty man...*It was absolutely diabolical, shot through with the worst kind of schoolgirl-diary bathos. This happened whenever Janine tried to write these days. Whatever route she took she always ended up making an exhibition of her innermost thoughts and hang-ups.

She turned the page quickly and started over, this time limiting the narrative scope to the teddy bear and him alone. *Teddy was rather cross with me but I chose to ignore it.* Janine looked up and sucked the cap of her fountain pen. *In order to get him to smile I had to position him with his mouth turned fractionally to the left.* This was better. She wrote on in this vein for three quarters of a page and then read it back. A prickly sweat came over her. It was somehow even more obscenely personal than the previous page. This wasn't fiction: it was a true account of her relationship with Boris. The thought of other eyes seeing it made her cringe.

Driving to work, she had in mind something stylishly offbeat, which perhaps might be of interest to Harpers or Cosmopolitan. But anyone could see through this paper-thin artifice. Here was a story by a desperate and lonely woman about her loneliness and desperation. There was no way out, nothing she could do. Once again, she was caught in the labyrinth. And here, she decided, was a possible title for her story. In fact, she could even incorporate her new description of herself as a rider to the title. How about that for frankness and honesty?

Caught in the Labyrinth: A story about a desperately lonely woman written by a desperately lonely woman.

Even as she was writing this down in jest, another idea was looming up on its heels: a complex metaphysical scenario, more in the realms of science-fiction and fantasy than the everyday world. She saw the labyrinth itself as a physical entity – vast, sophisticated, infinitely complex, myriadly differentiated, but fundamentally *all the same*. It didn't matter what direction one took or where one happened to be, it was a total labyrinth one was caught in; and however hard one searched for a way out or for something non-labyrinthine, all one ever found was *more labyrinth*, more and more, forever and ever, without relief...

Now if she could incorporate this into a piece of writing, she could plot out her anxieties in symbolic form. It sounded good, but she'd been down this road before and had learnt such grandiose projects were too difficult, too much trouble. And anyway, what would writing it prove? The writing part wasn't a way out, it was once again merely a continuation of the initial syndrome – yet more of the labyrinth...

35

This was getting ridiculous. Janine put the cap on her pen, closed her pad and tossed them onto the coffee table.

Like most of the rest of the things in her life, her writing had run aground. By now, according to the plan, she should be on the verge of literary fame. But her magnum opus – the What-Went-Wrong-With-My-Marriage Novel – lay in her desk drawer, untouched for over two months, unfinished and probably unfinishable. Her marriage had been an insoluble crossword puzzle, and the novel intended to mirror this process had instead suffered the same fate. But the process didn't need a novel written about it – what went wrong with her marriage could be summed up in one sentence: Janine was too repressed, insular and career-centric to give David what he wanted, so he went off with someone who could supply those needs – warmth, a family atmosphere and ultimately children.

Of course, the narrator in Janine Bailey's novel didn't see it that way. *She* was the one in the right, the extoller of feminist virtues – freedom, independence and the right to a career – and the husband was the wimp who wanted 'a little woman to cook and clean and be a baby machine'. Janine liked rhyming sentences. The trouble with the novel was that Janine no longer believed this narrator: she had feet of clay and spoke with forked tongue. With hindsight Janine saw that a great deal of the novel was simply untrue. It sold a tragic breakdown of communication re-packaged as an escape from oppression. She knew it couldn't be true to life because now a year after the separation she was still oppressed! To make the novel viable, it would have to be completely re-written from this later perspective and Janine wasn't up to such a task. In fact, she wasn't even up to simple short stories...*Oh, help me Boris...*

The phone rang, making Janine start as she languished in her armchair. She looked at the clock: it was after ten. Who would be calling this late? Not her mother – she always phoned when Janine was eating. It was probably a wrong number...

'Hello...?'

36

There was no reply.

'Hello?' Janine repeated.

'...You've got lovely hair...'

'What?'

'Lovely hair and a lovely mouth...'

'Who is this?' Janine said, immediately recognising the voice of Geoff Hills.

'I want you to wave your silky hair all over my erect cock and then suck it off with your lovely red mouth.'

Janine looked at the receiver as though it had just turned into a live lobster, then she slammed it back into the cradle. The shock she experienced was a kind of suspended horror as if she'd just seen her hand sliced off by a circular saw but there hadn't yet been time for blood to spurt or pain to register. She felt numb and feathery and her heart was flapping like a hysterical bird. She needed a drink. There was a bottle of sherry on the sideboard, and Janine poured herself half a tumblerful. She was overcome with awe and incredulity. The rules had changed completely at a stroke. Hills had finally realised he would get nowhere by conventional methods, so instead he'd resorted to this. Well, the gloves were off now. Next time Janine saw him she would spit in his face.

By the following day, Janine had developed a lurid fascination for the murky underworld in which Hills's psyche dwelt. Strangely, she wanted to know more about him, wondering about the nature of his habits. Flashing in the park, perhaps? Molesting little girls? She was seriously intrigued by such questions. Did Hills indulge in hardcore pornography? Had he ever been with prostitutes? Was he into bondage and sadomasochism? Had he ever committed or attempted to commit an indecent assault? Was he a rapist, potential or actual? Like a biochemist tracking down a new killer virus, she needed information about her subject.

On one of her walks around the building, Janine steeled herself and chose a route which took her past the sales department. An element of daredevilry had crept into her behaviour. She was sufficiently angry to feel able to confront

Hills, while at the same time not having any clear idea of how she'd react to him face to face. Her heart drumming in her chest, she surveyed the main office from behind the safety of the glass partition. Hills was nowhere to be seen. But coming down the corridor towards her was Simon Llewellyn, who smiled when he got close enough.

'Hello, Janine. We don't often see you in this neck of the woods.'

'That's true...I just thought I'd take a different route to get back from PR to my office.'

Simon punched the air. 'That's the spirit! Be adventurous. Variety is the spice of life, eh?'

Janine remembered Simon's taste for this kind of inane workplace banter. 'Aye, you've got to take life by the scruff of the neck, Simon,' she replied in kind.

'You have that, Janine. You have that indeed...Only the other day, old Geoff Hills said to me, "Simon, you've got to live for the moment, boy. Life is not a rehearsal. This is it! Make the most of it while you can."'

Janine smiled. She could feel a useful moment coming up. 'Quite a character, Geoff, isn't he?'

'Oh, he is that. No mistake.'

Janine looked at Simon's moustache; it reminded her of RAF pilots' wings. 'I haven't seen him around today.'

'No, you wouldn't. He's away doing a blitz of the North. Won't be back this week.'

This was it – her opportunity to discover Hills's *status*. His records said he was married, but then so did hers...

'He isn't leaving some lonely wife waiting for him at home, is he?' Listening to the words make a sequenced exit from her mouth, she knew she'd made a mistake.

'Geoff? Nooooo...He's not married. Oh no. Separated.' Simon winked at her. 'Like you.'

Janine's head felt suddenly hot as if it had just been microwaved. She excused herself and scuttled back to her office. How many other people knew of Hills's interest in her? It was probably the main talking point of the sales office. At this very moment Simon Llewellyn was no doubt

38

filling in the other reps on the latest. 'She took a detour to go past the office and look for him. When she saw me, she asked if he was *married*. Geoff's in there alright – the lucky bugger!' Janine banged her fists on the desk. She felt like throwing crockery or kicking in a plate glass window.

Men! It was pointless choosing between them because fundamentally they were all the same. And they stuck together, backed each other up like members of a secret society. Roll up, boys. All you need to join is an erect cock! Women were not classified as persons from this standpoint. They were merely the possessors, the custodians of the sexual apparatus necessary to enable *it* to take place – 'it' being contact as a quantifiable commodity, like money. It had its roots in teenage petting, and Janine remembered the demotic of her male contemporaries...Two points for a hand on a tit, three for a suck of a nipple, five for a hand in the knickers, and ten for a finger inside the cunt – a 'fish finger' as they called it with their delightful sense of style and savoir faire. When they graduated into adults, they played the same game for higher stakes. Fifty points for screwing Randy Mandy in the typing pool – she was a good sport and would do it with practically anybody, so that wasn't much of a challenge. A hundred points for Deborah in Public Relations – she was still a goer but a bit classier with it; you had to wine her and dine her well before she'd let you have your oats. And what about Janine, the ice-maiden, the boss's personal assistant? Five hundred – no a thousand – points if you could get the kecks off that one...To boldly go where no known man has been before – now that would be a supreme achievement...'Go for it, Geoff! We're right behind you, mate. But afterwards we want to know *all* the details...'

Janine imagined Hills grinding and grunting on top of her like a prize pig, finally depositing his seed – if he didn't wear a condom – in her inner sanctum. Another conquest. Another notch on the gun barrel. But what was *she* supposed to get out of it? Did he ever stop for one second and consider her point of view? Perhaps he thought she *liked* being harassed on a daily basis and then subjected to dirty talk? Janine shook her head. The minds of men...they were unfathomable.

Two days later, Janine received another late-night phone call from Hills. As soon as she knew it was him, she slammed the phone down and left it off the hook. His strategy was clear: while he was away up North, he couldn't be challenged by her in the daytime. What a brutal, disgusting bully he was! Janine could see him flopped out on the bed of his hotel, having his bit of fun with the phone before going out to a disco with other reps and trying to pick up tarts...

This business was ruining her life. She could consider nothing else except her anger and contempt towards this man. There was a hard edge, a fighting edge to her now, which she felt had developed to protect an ever-weakening centre. She was sleeping badly and felt tired throughout the day. Her head was full of noise, male noise: bar room chatter and ribald laughter – directed at her. She wanted to turn it off like the television, but there was no switch. In addition, she'd developed an unhealthy suspicion of phones – any phone, any place. Janine felt vulnerable and exposed: she experienced herself as a hapless and helpless victim.

Many times, she considered the courses of action available to take against Hills. She could report him to the police or the company personnel manager. Sexual harassment was taken more seriously these days. But all any official body would do was question Hills who would just deny it. He might even turn around and accuse her of trying to blacken his name. There would be a scandal, and everyone in the company would get to hear about it. Basically, Janine was hampered by a lack of concrete proof. If she could get the calls *recorded* that might help. It was all so tortuous. The easiest thing would be to get the number changed and go ex-directory.

At nine o'clock on Sunday night, after Janine had spent a particularly depressing weekend – Abigail had gone away with her boyfriend and Janine had seen no one – the phone rang, and she knew it had to be Hills again. This time she wasn't going to slam it down.

'Yes?'

'Guess what...? I've got my cock out now – it's in my hand...I want you to *go down* on it. *Suck* it. Take it *deep* into your throat...'

Again, Janine had that feeling of ghost-train tension and thrill – fascinated expectancy and horror combined. She had to keep hold of herself, wait for the moment, and then strike back.

'...I can feel your mouth around the shaft now, gripping it tight...your tongue slithering around the head...Mmmn, tasty, eh?'

'Look, I know who you are. I don't know if you think you're fooling me or what. Tomorrow I'm going to see the personnel manager and get advice about this. It's got to stop and it's going to stop. I'm putting the phone down now...'

Janine's heart was going incredibly fast and she was trembling significantly, but overall she felt she'd handled the situation well.

The following morning, she was at her desk early, psyching herself up for battle, preparing her speech to the personnel manager. At quarter past nine, she went to get a cup of coffee from the canteen, and on the way back she had a sudden rush of adrenalin. Why bother with the personnel manager? she thought. I'll go for Hills myself! She was worked up, on a roll, knew she could tackle him. It was now or never – she mustn't lose this moment and subside back into her usually depressive state. She had to get it sorted.

Janine tramped up the back stairs to the sales floor. When the bustling main office came into view behind the glass screen, she felt a stab of absolute panic and froze on the spot, unable to go forward or retrace her steps. Simon Llewellyn was on the other side of the glass, handing some papers to a secretary and giving her instructions. He glanced up, saw Janine, smiled and waved. The scene had the unreality of cinema; Janine had trouble believing she too was part of the action. Simon was coming to the door: he was going to speak to her!

'Here again, Janine? Can't keep away, can you? If you're looking for Geoff, you're too late, I'm afraid.'

41

'Where is he...?' Her voice had a disembodied, drugged quality.

Simon looked at his watch. 'He should be out on the beach in Majorca by now, if he's got any sense.'

'Majorca...?'

Simon looked fully into Janine's face and his smile was momentarily displaced by concern. 'Yes...Some of the boys organised a package trip – cheap rates for a block booking, you know the kind of thing. Well, there was a spare place and Geoff came in on Friday afternoon and snapped it up there and then. He had leave owing to him so he took it. Said he needed a bit of excitement in his life...'

'When did they fly?' Janine said.

Simon eyed her quizzically. 'Um...Sunday night...'

'What was the flight time?'

The flight time...? Let's see...about eight pm...That's right, they had to check-in at six to fly at eight – and the airport was Gatwick, if you want to...Hey, are you alright? You've gone white as a sheet. Do you want to come in and sit down?'

'No...thank you, Simon. I just felt a little light-headed, I'm fine now, really...'

Janine returned to her office in a kind of dream. She felt dazed and bewildered – mildly shocked as though she'd just been in an accident. It amazed and stunned her that her mind was capable of travelling so far and so purposefully in a totally spurious direction. She conjectured a scene where instead of meeting Simon Llewellyn she'd met Hills and accused him to his face. It could so easily have happened. The prospect made her wince to the marrow. Yet it wasn't totally her fault. She had good reason to be in a state of confusion. The man at the other end of the phone may not have been Hills, but he certainly was *somebody*.

A wave of chilled horror caressed her stomach. So...who was this person? Did he know her? Or did he find her by a random process? Janine strained to remember the content of the calls. He talked of silky hair and red lips – she *did* have silky hair and favoured red lipstick, though since the calls she'd taken to wearing peach! Therefore, it looked likely this person either knew her or at least knew what she looked like. The latter seemed the most likely; having eliminated Hills, she could think of no other candidates for the former. To find her phone number, this person would need to know her surname and her address. It could be someone who lived locally who'd seen her coming and going...but how would he know the name? A casual enquiry to her immediate neighbours...a glance at a newspaper sticking out of the letterbox with 'Bailey' scrawled on it...There were a thousand ways.

The important thing was the matter was now definitely outside the sphere of the company, so she should inform the police. But by the end of the working day, she hadn't yet done so. It seemed like an enormous chore for which she had to muster unreachable reserves of strength. All she wanted to do now was rest; this affair had exhausted her. Though once she was back inside the four walls of home, her daze did not subside into relaxation as she'd hoped, but instead gave way to dread. In the workplace a protective layer existed; here she was fully exposed to the inevitable, the horror...the phone ringing once again.

Janine went through the motions of preparing and eating her supper, then she watched Coronation Street, a documentary about polluted rivers and the news. All the time she was painfully aware she *was* going through the motions, that she was really a soldier in a war zone waiting for the enemy to strike. By ten o'clock she could feel the anxiety coming to a peak. She told herself not to lose her grip. A phone call couldn't actually *hurt* her; she mustn't *exaggerate* the danger in her own mind. But her mind was the tool with which she perceived the world: if it chose to make things appear *bigger*, then as far as her reality was concerned, they were *actually bigger...*

To make things worse, she could hear a mischievous voice in the back of her head insinuating that she actually *liked* the content of the calls...You want more, don't you? Love every minute of it. Can't get enough...*That's silly*, Janine thought by way of reply. After several minutes of this, she was locked

43

in a loop where both the accusations and her defences against them repeated incessantly, gaining in pace and menacing effect. Now she was not only being terrorised by a stranger on the phone, but also by her own psyche. She realised the organization of things was set against her decisively: someone up there didn't like her. It wasn't her choice that Hills should chase her or this man should phone, but she felt rebuked as though it was – as though she'd somehow instigated it all, and now it was her responsibility to find a way out...or else.

She was starting to seriously scare herself now, and at the same time she recognised this as the syndrome by which things were made worse still. Again, she considered calling the police and registering a complaint. But she was way beyond that; she couldn't trust herself to speak and act logically. *This* knowledge brought her to the verge of a full-blown panic attack. Vainly she tried to 'unthink' the thoughts which had paved the way, discovering to her additional alarm that thinking doesn't possess a reverse gear...

Calm down, Janine. Don't panic...No, no. Do something to take your mind off things...

Mechanically, she went to her desk and got a magazine to read. The journey there and back served as further proof of the strange state she had entered. She felt disassociated from her body to the point where she'd become a kind of spectator to her own actions. Her legs did the job of locomotion, and her hands gripped as they should, but it was hard to believe that she herself was actually involved in the neurological command structure. Doubt on this primary level was the portal of madness...Janine felt a pang of pure terror. She tried to read, but her mind couldn't gain traction with the content of any of the articles. Eventually she let the magazine fall into her lap, and she just lay back in the armchair, trying to breathe as slowly as possible.

At ten forty-five the phone rang, and Janine listened to it ring fifteen, perhaps twenty times before she rose to answer it like a sleepwalker summoned to the gallows.

'Hello...?'

'You think you know who I am – but you *don't* know who I am...I know who you are though...You're a tasty bit of stuff with blonde hair and red lips...'

No, it wasn't Hills's voice. The pitch was similar – a mid-baritone – but the accent was quite different.

'...I bet you've got dark pubes, haven't you...? I love girls with blonde hair and dark pubes...Bet you've got a big juicy one too, eh? Like a bacon sandwich all wet and dripping with fat...ha, ha, ha, ha, ha...'

Janine snorted an involuntary laugh. 'If you could only hear how silly you sound,' she said. 'You must be totally sick – an inadequate, pathetic little shit to have to do this. I feel sorry for you – I really do...'

There was silence for about four seconds, then Janine heard a click at the other end of the line. *He'd* put the phone down this time. What did it mean? She went to the kitchen to get a drink of mineral water. As she watched her hands pour the liquid into a glass, the sense of them not belonging to her was stronger than ever...She'd made him *angry* now. Even before her mind could run the sequence properly, her body was registering the emergency...

This was no everyday man; this was a *pervert* who probably had a history of violence. He was no doubt local and knew where she lived...*He could be making his way here at this very moment!* She had to phone the police immediately – dial 999. She sipped the water and quickly tried to formulate a credible account of the events. Version after version speeded through her mind like a tape in fast forward, the content of each new attempt merging and blending with the old to create an amorphous splurge of language. She was flapping too much. It was *imperative* that she organise the information properly. But before she could get much further, she heard a noise in the backyard – a small flowerpot perhaps, falling onto the path with a light thud, only a few feet beyond the back door where she stood. She froze and listened. Shortly there was a scuffling sound, and then some bamboo poles rattling. Someone was moving around out there, but it was too dark for him to see where he was going.

The kitchen light was off, but the space was partially lit by the strong hall light coming through the open doorway. If Janine moved into the light to make a dash for the phone, he would easily see her through the curtainless window. He could kick the door in and grab her before she had a chance to dial. It was safest to remain where she was by the door, concealed by reasonable shadow.

Janine was too petrified to risk the slightest movement – even to breathe seemed reckless. As moment followed moment, she formed vivid visions of what a struggle would be like...The muscular arms forcing her to the ground with effortless superiority of strength...the intruding knee pushing her legs apart...the purposeful fingers tearing at her clothing...the big fist ready to pound her face if she put up any resistance...Her heart accelerated till she thought it would burst out of her chest. She realised with total panic that now there was no longer anything mooring her to the shoreline of normal everyday living: one by one the ropes had frayed and snapped and now she was all on her own. The events which had led up to this point – her sour marriage, the separation, the failed attempt to write about it or put anything in its place, the fiasco with Hills, the dirty phone calls – replayed themselves in lurid quick-fire flashback to confirm the certainty that fate had chosen and shaped her to be a victim. All of it was *real*, and it looked totally catastrophic. She knew this was the night she was meant to perish...

Janine heard a distinct groan, and it was a second before she realised it had come from her own mouth. It was a sign she had finally exhausted all possibilities for control over what was happening. This was overload...breaking point. She felt her defences give way like a bursting dam.

The propulsion for the scream came from somewhere very deep in the pit of her stomach. It rose upwards like a missile and connected with her vocal centres, exploding into life. It filled her ears, her brain, her whole being. Janine screamed without restraint, without inhibition. She *was* screamed – the scream was in charge, not her. Every cell in her body and every ounce of her strength were participating in the scream.

46

Her mouth was open so wide it stretched her lips to the limit of their elasticity, and her jaw felt on the point of dislocation. In the middle of it all, she registered the impact of something hitting against the door, and through the window she saw a large bushy-tailed fox scamper across the terrace, pause and look back in her direction, then jump onto the fence and disappear.

As the scream exhausted its energy, it automatically subsided into deep sobbing. Janine cried differently from usual – she cried with the same lack of control and total emotional spillage as a young child. In fact, she was stripped down to the point of feeling the precise helplessness and vulnerability of such a young child. She felt pathetic and silly and shamed – above all shamed. But it didn't matter because everything was all right now. Even as she was experiencing them, these negative emotions were floating away from her to be replaced by something she recognised as serenity.

Janine sat down at the table and finished the mineral water. She relaxed and tuned into her heart as it quietened like a decelerating engine. The night held no terrors. Her tormentor was gone and a newly revealed moon had turned the garden enchantingly surrealistic. Apparently no one had heard the noise.

Janine's body was filled with a new warmth and vibrancy. She could feel it tingling in her fingertips, soothing her alimentary canal, and gripping her cerebral cortex like a warm, comfortable skullcap. She felt curiously better connected than she had for any time in recent memory. The problems which had weighed on her so heavily now seemed tamer – domesticated cats instead of ferocious jungle beasts. Dirty phone callers were minor league players; it was unlikely that one would rush around to do violence on the strength of a rebuff. Nevertheless, she would still give the police a full account of what had happened and get her number changed...

And what about Hills...? Janine chuckled. Poor old Geoff – she'd done him an injustice. He was just a newly single guy trying a bit too hard to re-circulate himself. It was no more

47

sinister than that. She sympathised with him, even wished to be more friendly with him – on a platonic basis, of course.

It never failed to intrigued Janine Bailey...the way the mind could leap off and build false constructions, then do its utmost to bolster and solidify them till they completely swamped the true version. But there was no stopping the mind – it was something to do with the way the neurons were wired together in the brain. People inflict pain on themselves and on others, and would continue doing so, never knowing except for perhaps a brief instant, or the duration of a rare peak experience such as this one that it was all fundamentally unnecessary.

ALL THE KING'S HORSES

*W*hy did she have to leave me?

I've been asking myself that question all day at work and trying to prevent the anger from showing – I mustn't go berserk and ruin my work life as well as my personal one. But whatever I do I feel the pressure there like a steam hammer, pounding on the doors of my resistance, ready to smash itself free at any moment.

I'm driving home now, and every last thing is making me angry – there is nothing that is *not* making me angry. A traffic light on a pelican crossing turns amber and I have to stop. I mutter curses at the stupid bumptious housewife responsible – who does she think she is? One person holding up a whole stream of traffic like this? And the way she walks! – slowly and regally like the bloody Queen Mother! *Gettafucking move on!*

I found the note from Joanna, my wife, yesterday evening when I got in. It said something like: *I can't stand your disgusting temper a moment longer, I'm going away to have a life of my own, etcetera.* She can't stand my temper, so she goes and does something which makes my temper TEN TIMES WORSE! That's typical of her – the stupid selfish despicable bitch! Always thinking of herself, that's all she ever does, never of me...

Urrrggghhhh!!! I can feel the steam hammer pounding again.

There's a cretin in front of me who's sticking rigidly to the 30 miles per hour speed limit – not a mile above it, nor a mile below it. WANKER! I could have overtaken in the turning-right lane back there if only I'd sussed him out, but I didn't try because he's got a Peugeot 205 GTI, and they go like shit. He drives it like it's a bleeding hearse! And now I'm stuck behind the fucker while there's miles of clear road ahead. Still, I'll have him at the next lights...

Okay, so I hit Joanna a couple of days back – harder than ever before. But she asked for it! If ever a woman was asking to be walloped, by God it was her...She *knows* I don't like her fraternising with other men, she *knows* it winds me up; yet she went ahead and did it – blatantly! It was supposed to be her 'night out with the girls' – a night out behaving like a complete scrubber, more like. When she was picked up, I followed her at a discreet distance, tracking the group to the Coach and Horses where there was a live band. I kept in the shadows and watched as she and her friends were chatted-up by three men whom they obviously knew; then the six of them went off and danced together, doing those crotch-grinding type gyrations.

I'd seen enough; I had to restrain myself from going up and fisting Joanna right there in the pub. Instead, I went home fuming and waited for her to put in an appearance. It was after one o'clock when she finally got in, and by then I was way past wanting a verbal confrontation; I just let her have it with kitchen stool the moment she was through the door. Between blows I told her I'd followed her and what I'd seen. After it was over and she was cleaning herself up, she said it was all 'innocent' and no more than 'a bit of fun'. Huh! I was actually expected to believe that shit.

I made a right mess of one side of her face; the next day she had an eye like a stewed plum, raw bruises on her forehead and cheekbone, and lips like an inflatable life raft. That'll teach her, I thought.

I'm stopped at the lights now, in the outside lane parallel with the Peugeot, ready to beat him to the point where the two lanes merge into one. Red and amber, here we go. I accelerate hard, but he's doing the same. I go flat out and he's still up with me, determined to keep me from getting past. I'm being squeezed into the path of the oncoming traffic; I've no choice but to drop back...

Oh no! I don't believe this – now he's slowed back down to 30. The fucking little CUNT! This guy obviously belongs to the Joanna school of winding me up!

We reach the dual carriageway leading to the ring road.

Here the speed limit is 50, and as expected fuck-features keeps to it exactly. I zoom past him at around 75 – there's no speed cameras on this stretch – and can't resist giving him a big fat middle finger as I do so. I cross the roundabout and take the long dual stretch to the next suburb, overtaking everything at around 85, putting as much distance between me and that bastard as possible.

I'm going past a big lorry, nearing the next roundabout when my rear-view mirror fills with a fast car, pressing to get through. It looks like a Peugeot, but it can't be him – he obeys speed limits. I pass the lorry and pull into the nearside lane, but keep going as fast as safety allows into the roundabout – just in case. He's racing me now, neck and neck, and I see it is him; he's abandoned all his 'rules' in the effort to get back at me.

We hit the roundabout, and he's slightly in front, but I crash into third and hammer towards my exit. He hugs the middle at reckless speed, then literally forces himself in front of me. I have two choices: I can either brake and let him in, or carry on and collide with his rear wing. I almost do the latter, but capitulate in the end. Then he slows right back down to 30 again – even though there's no limit on this stretch!

I'm not having this! I'M JUST NOT HAVING THIS! He thinks he's won; well, we'll see about that...

I drive as close as I can to his rear bumper, then I drop back and cannon towards him, stopping just short each time. I put on my fog lamps and headlamps on full beam. I'm going to follow the bastard home, that's what I'm going to do. I'll find out where he lives, then I'll petrol-bomb his house in the dead of night. *Yeeess!* Don't think I won't, either. They'll be nothing to trace it to me, no discernible motive. The perfect crime.

This guy must be very brave, I'll hand that to him. Doesn't he know he's dealing with a desperate man? Can't he tell I've got nothing to lose? It's true! Now that Joanna's gone, I can look forward to an endless stream of nights coming home to an empty house, weekends on my own, the monotony of the local pub on my own. I'll remain incarcerated in the prison of my own isolation till I die. *Grrrr!*

I'm not paying attention; the traffic has concertinaed together and unexpectedly someone brakes three cars ahead. I can't stop in time and I smash into the back of Shitface in the Peugeot. It seems unreal – I can't believe that he's pushed me so far; that he's made me lose control of my driving. It's a fucking disgrace! I bow my head, a feeling like death building inside me.

The guy's getting out of his car now and he looks angry, reminding me of one of my old teachers from schooldays. HE is angry at ME? He's caused this whole debacle – first by driving too slowly, then by driving too fast – and now he wants to get *angry* about it into the bargain? Oh yeah? I'll show him what anger is.

With rocket fuel thumping through my veins, I reach behind to the back seat and take hold of my Stoplock anti-theft device, snapping shut the head unit which clamps onto the steering wheel. I feel like I'm in a movie and watching it at the same time. Out I get, brandishing the thing and I see his expression turn from indignation to fear. That's the way I like it. I'm a vastly superior being to him; I can take risks and operate on a level he can't even begin to contemplate. Whatever he does I'll go one better – I'll up the stakes to the limit. No compromise.

Now I'm possessed by a terrific feeling – it's as if I've stripped from my body a suit of rules about how you should act, and I'm running naked into a primal freedom where you JUST DO WHAT YOU WANT TO DO!

As I come closer, the guy stands square and holds up his hand like a policeman trying to stop traffic.

'Put it down,' he says slowly and with irritation as though addressing a naughty child. 'Put it down on the ground now. Don't be stupid...'

STUPID? On top of everything else he's now CALLING ME STUPID? STUPIIIIIIIIIIIIIIIIDDD!!!

I lunge with the Stoplock and catch him hard on the lower jaw, making him recoil and cower, covering his face with his arms. No one – nothing on earth – can derail the express train of my wrath now. Not all the king's horses, nor all the king's men...

I swing back the Stoplock two-handed like a golf club and bring it down with all my strength on the back of his head...

WHY NOT? WHAT HAVE I GOT TO LOSE?

He falls forward across the bonnet of his flash car and slumps onto the road. Now I take the Stoplock in two hands and hammer it down onto his head. Once. Twice. Three times...

GO FOR BROKE! FUCK IT!

His head is changing shape like dough...

The sight of an edge of bone protruding through blood and hair brings me back into myself, and I get a nasty flash of the seriousness of things. I hear traffic and murmuring voices; I see a bus pull up ahead and people disembark. The normalcy of these things framing this abnormal event starts to make me panicky.

I look down at the guy, hoping he won't be there; but no luck. He is motionless – apart from one hand, which exhibits a high-frequency trembling that brings home the concept of brain injury very graphically. A raspberry jam mess is oozing out of the side of his head, and as I watch it consolidates into a gurgling and bubbling like volcanic lava.

Did *I* do that...?

Now I stare at the cracked and blood-smeared Stoplock in my hands. The anger has drained and that suit of rules is fitting itself back into place. I'd like to get in my car, go home and pretend it never happened; but dozens of people are clustered on the street watching me, and I hear the distant whine of a police siren. I want to explain to everyone that it wasn't my fault. I did it because I felt so bad that it seemed impossible I could feel any worse, no matter what I did, therefore I may as well do *anything* – it didn't matter.

But shit...! Face facts, for fucksake. A man is badly injured, perhaps dead. *Someone* must be responsible...

'Joanna,' I say, shaking my head, 'you've got a lot to answer for.'

THE PHOTOGRAPHER

Debbie, my best friend of schooldays, would always say this to me whenever I told her of my latest boy troubles:

'Penelope, it's your own fault. You keep on picking such dickheads to get involved with.'

And I would reply: 'They don't seem like dickheads to start with. I don't do it on purpose – it just works out that way.'

Now a decade or more after these conversations I've discovered to my cost that my instincts haven't improved. No matter how good a man looks on the surface, seemingly he will turn out, on closer inspection, to be a prize-winning dud. But how can one know this for sure unless one carries out that closer inspection? Be fair, there is no other way. And Roland did look an extremely promising bet...

When I first saw him, I felt him to be an actual creation of my thoughts and longings who, by some amazing magical process, had stepped clear of my head to become flesh and blood. After six years in a frustrating marriage, much of it spent searching for a new ship from which to fly my colours, I knew immediately he was *the one*. It's weird how these things happen right on cue, as if ordained by a higher power. Just when I'd hit a real low point, just when I needed him the most, suddenly there he was! – all six feet four of him, getting out of his ink-blue Mercedes 500 SL in the car park of Redhill Sports and Social Club.

It was early evening and I was on my way home to prepare dinner for Keith, my husband. Roland's car door clunked – an expensive, well-engineered German clunk – and he shouldered his kit bag and ambled right towards me. I smiled and he smiled back. There was empathy and ease between us from this very first moment.

I liked his height immediately because it signified authority, but I noticed with approval that his other proportions were nicely scaled-down. His hips were narrow and he was very slender, though his straight back and square shoulders prevented him from looking gangly or willowy. He had a round boyish face, and his hair, though prematurely greying, was youthful in style – full and fringed, covering the ears, wispy at the back. It made a pleasing contrast with his deeply tanned skin and huge mysterious grey-green eyes. The lines of his cheekbones, his jaw and his nose were sharp and ideally proportioned as in a bust of a Roman emperor or a portrait of a sixteenth century Spanish nobleman. He was exotic, larger than life – *better* than life.

The moment I saw him I went weak and delirious with desire like a child who wakes to a stack of presents on Christmas morning, and thinks: *At last!*

He looked into my eyes as we passed and said, 'Hello,' totally naturally in a deep rich commanding voice, still keeping up his fresh smile. I said hello back, then turned to study his rear aspect retreating towards the building. I was thinking I must have forgotten something back in the changing rooms. Surely...I searched my bag in a pantomime designed to convince myself. I wasn't about to get into my car and go home to Keith at a time like this.

I met my Keith at university. He was a third-year law student, and I an English Lit. second year. Naturally he looked good on the surface: tastefully dressed, well behaved, with all the other trappings of a reasonably cultured background. I found him a refreshing change from the usual campus male, whose idea of a great night out was to drink fifteen pints of Newcastle Brown while listening to ear-liquefying heavy metal, then come back to your room for coffee and be sick all over your bed. Keith and I started going out to pubs and restaurants and the cinema together, and within three weeks we were having regular sex.

Actually, he was only the third guy I'd ever been to bed with, and the other two were nothing to rave about. The first was a medical student I met at the freshers' ball. I didn't even like him much – I was only drawn into it out of a neurotic idea that I was the only virgin in my intake, and I had to put that to rights immediately. At the end of a dreadful two weeks with this medical man I required medical attention: he'd given me a nasty little present called NSU.

My second encounter was no more rewarding. It consisted of a one-night-stand with my tutor, who by virtue of the speed of his performance must have been suffering from premature ejaculation, or something very close to it. Still, this was better than my old sixth form boyfriend, Malcolm, who simply couldn't get an erection. No matter how hard he tried all he managed was to get redder and redder in the face. I lied to Debbie for three months about the great sex we were having before tearfully I had to admit the truth.

So, at the time Keith was something of a saviour. He was my first real lover, and naturally he seemed great because I had nothing worthwhile to compare him to. And, of course, we fell in love. Yes, why push it into the background? We admitted it to each other at the end of the second month, and the consequences were obvious to us both. When you consider what I was then – an apathetic English student who'd read hardly any of the set books and for understandable reasons was giving tutorials a wide berth! – marriage to Keith represented a way out, a passport to a new life.

He proposed to me just before the big push to his final exams. I didn't take any time to think it over, I cheerfully agreed to give up my academic career and follow him back to his home town where a job was waiting for him at a long-established firm. And so, at the tender age of twenty I became Mrs Penelope Burke, wife of Keith Burke, solicitors' clerk. Taking on a name like that you'd think I might have been a little wary, seen it as a sign of things to come, wouldn't you?

My stomach airborne like a hovercraft, I sneaked back into the club, and careful not to be seen, I watched Roland at play. In the next few days, I made discreet enquiries and found out he was a top fashion and advertising photographer who worked primarily in London, where he had a flat, but also sometimes at the studio at his house down here. His time was split about fifty-fifty, and when he was here, he usually visited the club in the early evening for a game of squash and a swim. I attended every evening possible to maximise my chances of seeing him. Keith thought I was turning into a fitness fanatic. Roland always played with the same friend, Gregory Dawes, a lawyer whom Keith knew vaguely. So far there was no sign of a woman in his life.

Over the weeks my habit of ritual voyeurism coupled with its attendant fantasisation came to dominate my waking moments. I drank in Roland's grace and coordination on the court – the thin but muscular brown arms and legs, lightly haired, flashing like the levers on a complex machine. And in the pool, where I could mingle with him without arrangement, I drank in the taut exquisitely toned stomach, the small nipples mounted on the spare domes of his pectorals, the minute ass, the long grey-brown hair, wet and slicked back, giving him at times a slightly Tarzan-like aspect.

In reciprocation I paraded myself for him with a precisely calibrated effect – not in too obvious and pushy a way like a tart, but enough to show him that here was a voluptuous woman who considered herself his peer. After aerobics I sauntered about the premises in my Lycra leotard and tights like a lynx on the prowl, coolly aware of turning masculine heads which included Roland's when my timing was right. In the pool I wore my new cutaway black bikini, an almost non-existent creation held together precariously with gold links. The skimpy top underpinned and compressed my breasts to their best advantage, and as I brushed by Roland, giving him the faintest of casual smiles, I was conscious of walking like a model – head erect, lungs full, feet close together, almost like walking a tightrope.

As for the bikini bottom, I had to crop and shave my pubic hair practically to nothing to stop it from sprouting out of the sides. While I was doing it, I imagined Roland watching me and conjectured his approval. I was becoming more and more rampant by the day.

At the dawn of my marriage, I naively envisaged a comfortable life ahead of me. With Keith as the breadwinner, I could simply lead a life of leisure, doing exactly as I pleased, spending his hard-earned money. Or so I thought. Vacuuming and cleaning our Georgian-style detached house – bought partially with a loan from Keith's parents – was fun for about half the first week, as was shopping at Waitrose and preparing exotic suppers for when Keith came home. But it soon dawned on me that I would have to *go on* doing this in perpetuity, always the same tasks in a similar way for as long as I lived – or as long as I stayed married. Keith sometimes helped with the cooking and cleaning; that wasn't the problem. It was the nightmarish predictability of everything: the knowledge that short of a nuclear war nothing would significantly change – ever. That was the problem – *and* Keith's parents. Oh, my God...

It was sheer murder. They came around to our house virtually every other day on some pretext or another, or else we were summoned to theirs. Keith's father was a retired naval officer, a *commodore* who'd retained this form of address as a title in civilian life. He was a stout, barrel-chested, bullish man who'd been used to giving orders all of his life and wasn't about to stop now. Keith's mother was an equally stolid old-fashioned-style wife who echoed and amplified everything her husband said. Right from the start the pecking order was clear. The Commodore was in supreme command with Mrs Burke as first officer; Keith was the ensign or sub-lieutenant, and I was the 'other ranks', the cabin boy.

Because the Burkes dominated Keith without question, they automatically assumed the right to dominate me. In our home it would be: 'Why don't you move that lamp out of the corner, Penelope...the light will *spread* better.' At sea, aboard the Commodore's yacht, the predicament was the same: 'Pull that sheet in, girl! Don't just stand there like a dummy.' And later: 'Whatsamatter? Feeling a little *gippy*, are we? Ha, ha, ha. Don't worry, you'll soon get your sea legs.' And in the Lake

District half way up a famous mountain, with new boots turning my feet to mincemeat, I would hear: 'Get a move on, Penelope. You're making us behind schedule. I know it's tough, but think of it as *character-building*. You'll be a better person as a result of this experience.'

All crap – the lot of it!

As you can imagine, this 'new life' was an incredible shock to my system. There was nowhere to run for relief – I was in a strange town where I knew no one; I was hundreds of miles away from the support of my own family and friends, my bridges truly incinerated. But the greater shock came from seeing Keith, the man I married, just lying back and taking all this as though it was a perfectly natural way to live.

I remember vividly a certain moment when I suddenly saw him in a new light. He looked so small, so unimportant, so *meaningless* as a human being. As he jumped up and down saying, 'Okay, Dad...You're *right*, Mum,' I felt as though I'd walked in through the wrong door and I shouldn't be here – this wasn't a part of *my* life at all! But no matter how many times I blinked or pinched myself it didn't go away. This *was* my life, and it had reached the point where abandoning ship, as I'd done at university, was no longer a viable option.

It was when Roland invaded my dreams that I was absolutely sure this infatuation was real. We came across each other in this huge subterranean amphitheatre on an iron gangway suspended over water. I was escaping from some people – a gang of Nazis, I think. Roland took my hand and led me upstairs into a kind of super-plush department store, where he took it upon himself to re-attire me. First, he found this exquisite red velvet evening dress and displayed it for my approval like he'd designed it himself. After I'd put it on, together with some black stockings, I sat down and Roland slipped my feet into black patent four-inch heels.

Beyond the window I saw our white Lear jet waiting on the taxiway. Roland lifted my arm and I stood up and fell into his embrace. When he kissed me, it was all-consumingly delicious and oh so realistic. At that point I woke up, wanting more but unable to keep the dream going. I had to have more. It was *love*, and here was the proof I needed.

I suppose it must happen to everyone at some time in the course of married life. A person with a happy and prosperous marriage would probably fend off the situation, avoid seeing the person and try to minimalize future disruption. But for someone like myself who'd been systematically sexually undernourished for just about all of her life, the temptation was irresistible. I'd fallen so far behind in the Love Race that an affair with someone like Roland represented my only real chance to catch up again.

Moreover, if we got together, I would not only have a dream man at last, but also I'd be socially elevated into the circles I knew I was meant to inhabit. They'd be parties in posh London houses, impromptu trips to desert islands and far-away cities, fabulous festivals where we'd rub shoulders with the rich and famous. My success would secure the future, and also make *the past* all right too by putting it in a proper context – a preparation for all this.

But my fantasies and aspirations were running way ahead of the real scene. Nothing had happened yet beyond mutual eyeing-up and the exchange of perfunctory greetings and small-talk. I'd thought Roland a cool customer for not taking things further himself, but I was forgetting – I was a married woman with hunks of gold on her significant finger. Roland was not the sort of guy to make a pass at a married woman – of course not! I had to break the ice and show him *I* was interested. It was an awesome responsibility, like staking all of one's life savings on the turn of a roulette wheel.

By now I was making myself nervous and butterflies brushed my insides whenever I considered this task – now unavoidable – and all the complications and potential pitfalls it encompassed. I realised I'd started something, and I had to stay with it, developing my approach as it escalated. Posing around the pool was okay in the early stages, but it was fast becoming monotonous to continue it without accompaniment. The rest of the orchestra had to be brought into play.

*   *   *   *

After about three years of marriage, whatever small interest I retained in sex had completely evaporated. Keith and I had tried all the positions, all the permutations countless times, and now the only 'innovation' left was to avoid the whole process as much as possible because it was so boring. Keith complained that I had a low sex drive, but this wasn't where the fault lay. The trouble with Keith was that he wasn't very good at *making love* – not just the sex part, but his whole approach. Keith didn't know how to stage manage that all important of ingredients – *an atmosphere*.

When I put this to him, he asked me what I wanted and I told him of my visions of doing it in four poster beds robed in satin sheets, of doing it in the shallows on moonlit beaches, of being swept off my feet and *romanced*. What I didn't say was these visions didn't include *him*. The truth was although I still *loved* Keith in a way, I no longer really *fancied* him.

Now I was a little older, I realised I'd been far too young to get married and commit myself to one bloke. I was due more experience. Keith was but a stage on a journey – not the final destination. The idea that my sex life would remain fixed at this point, that I would never have another man so long as I lived, seemed absurd. Keith was my first real lover and a necessary and important phase, but now it was time to move on.

Whenever Keith saw my restlessness, he interpreted it classically as 'sickening for something' – and what could that 'something' be other than children? Naturally the Commodore and Mrs B were in total agreement with this evaluation. My resistance to such notions led inevitably to arguments, which got pretty heated when the three of them ganged up against me. I took Keith aside and told him he'd better start supporting my point of view or else I'd walk out. He knew I meant it and for once he acted as a buffer between me and his parents.

My point of view was: 'There's plenty of time for all that stuff yet.' It sounded particularly lame coming from Keith's mouth.

Roland was usually still in the gym or the pool when I left, so in order to stand a chance of catching him unoccupied, I took to staying behind in the bar. Time passed slowly as I perched on a stool by my own pillar, gazing vacantly into an orange juice and fizzy water.

The people I knew were strictly a day set – housewives, pensioners and other non-workers – and the evening crowd were largely strangers to me. In my isolation I felt conspicuous and self-conscious, loaded down with the guilt of a child who knows its motives are entirely transparent to the adult onlooker.

After two fruitless nights, I was sobered and humbled, ready to abandon the entire quest on the grounds of its silliness. Then on the third night Roland came in with Gregory and two others. They were all laughing and joking together the way men do, but when Roland saw me, a flash of interest crossed his face and he instantly gave me his attention. Sparks flew inside me as that special electricity began to surge and my stomach was airborne again. I had to keep calm and not make myself look ridiculous.

'All on your own?' I heard him say.

'Oh, yes...' I replied, showing my nearly empty glass. 'Just topping up on the vitamin C.'

'Let me get you another,' he said.

We talked about the club, the facilities, the people; how the weather had turned suddenly hot and our expectations of a good summer. All the time I was thinking *This is it – it's happening!* and I felt so relieved the exam was finally underway and the questions weren't too difficult after all.

Following the first round of banter there was a small lull, and I said, 'What do you do?'

'I'm a photographer,' he said.

'That's interesting...What are you working on at the moment?'

'A series of still lives for a cosmetics company.'

'Do you do that here or in London?'

'I discuss the brief with the art director in London, but I do the actual work at my studio in my back garden. You're welcome to see it sometime if you're interested.'

'Thank you, I'm very interested. I once thought of becoming a model – you use models as well, I take it?'

'Of course...' Roland looked at me candidly, then dropped his eyes to my hands. 'You're married, I see?'

'In a manner of speaking...'

Roland grinned expansively. Further discussion on this subject was unnecessary. Like I said, there was genuine empathy and understanding between us – I could hardly have foreseen what was about to happen.

'Look,' he said, 'not only do I take photographs, but I also like to cook and serve good wine. Why don't I collect you one night, give you the guided tour and some refreshment to boot?'

'That sounds marvellous,' I said, scarcely believing it had been so easy. We made an arrangement for the following week and said our *au revoirs*.

I drove home in a trance, singing snatches of old songs... 'Just One of Those Things'...'That Old Black Magic'...feeling I was in a movie cheek to cheek with Fred Astaire...

Even in the darkest hours of my marriage there always remained the possibility that one day I would shed all my inertia and hopelessness like an outgrown skin and emerge sleek and svelte, bathed and blow-dried, onto night's dance floor and have fun again. After our fourth anniversary, I decided I needed to get out of the house and meet more people, so I got myself a job as an assistant editor on a local listings magazine. Right from the outset this project had a hidden agenda: to be near men, to rub shoulders with men, and possibly engage in some form of dalliance with men.

I got friendly with a fair few in and around the office and out doing my reporting. They fuelled my fantasies which had the effect of improving my sex life with Keith for a while; but at this time no actual person presented as a suitable candidate for an affair. The nice guys were seemingly all in relationships, or acted as though they were. The ones who signalled their availability were either wimps, slap-and-tickle types, old, fat, or ugly – and often a combination of several of such factors.

Occasionally I'd bump into a guy who *was* sexually attractive *and* quite clearly willing, but then my heart would race like an alarm bell and I'd back away finding fault, making excuses to myself...*He's just a hustler out for a good time...You'd be making a slut of yourself, Penelope...If he'd sleep with you easily then he's probably got AIDS...*The ridiculous thing is I thought all *I* wanted was a good time – I certainly wasn't up to wrecking my marriage, not then anyway. The truth is despite all my earnestness I was too frightened and inhibited to take the plunge.

The day after I'd made the date with Roland, I hired the video of *Brief Encounter* and watched it on my own with the curtains closed. The poignancy was so strident, so deliciously heart-wrenching that I had tears in my eyes almost all the way through. I determined there and then that I wouldn't let Roland slip through my fingers as Celia Johnson had Trevor Howard. There was so much stacked against her, the poor thing. Women are always at their most disadvantaged and vulnerable when caught up in the mechanics of an affair.

And Celia Johnson didn't have to worry about AIDS.

Now that I was actually about to put my desires into practice, the picture was changing completely. A new and far more profound dread was creeping up to replace the old fear-of-failure anxiety. I was swamped by an urgent need to foresee problems and plan ahead...

Would Roland wear a condom automatically? If not what on earth do I do? Stop him and discuss the matter? Insist that he wear one? Carry some with me in case he doesn't have any of his own...? Would he then think me a slut for having a supply? If he refused to wear one, then this would increase the likelihood of him having AIDS. Panic surged through me when that old he's-just-a-hustler routine returned to mind.

And a new paranoia bloomed: the idea he wasn't just a hustler, he was also b-i-s-e-x-u-a-l.

Despite all potential hazards I was committed to going the distance with this one – no more hanging back. But I had to take precautions: however nice men may appear on the surface, you just don't know where they've *been*, do you?

Over six years had passed since the fateful day of my marriage by the time Roland came onto the scene. I'd been spending more and more time at Redhill, as the magazine had gone under through lack of advertising revenue. I was redundant – another victim of the recession. Still, my sojourn of work had largely served its purpose, obtaining for me a larger circle of friends and a degree of visibility within the community.

I would meet someone in the morning for a game of squash or tennis, then have a group lunch and later work out and swim. And if I felt like a lazy day, I could merely watch the energetic males striding about the courts with tendons taut and muscles pulsing, or streaking silver-backed through the water.

I needed as much diversion as possible, because on the home front the now's-the-time-to-have-children argument was coming to a head once again. Only days before first seeing Roland, I overheard this conversation between Keith and his father.

Keith: '...she'll come around. I'll work on it some more.'

The Commodore: 'That's what you always say, lad. But this stalling for time has gone on long enough. You must put your foot down. Have it out with her. After all she's *twenty-seven* now: she isn't getting any younger...'

Jesus! Twenty-seven and almost a write-off. Hearing this was enough to send me into major hysterics, except I basically agreed with Keith's father. Twenty-seven is old. I felt it just after my birthday. At twenty-six I was a senior young person; at twenty-seven I suddenly became a junior old person. I'd found the dividing line. Crossing it convinced me that the sand in the hour glass was indeed flowing, and I'd better do something fairly fast. Not have kids, of course, but get out of this hopeless claustrophobic marriage.

And just when I needed a catalyst, right at the moment when I'd decided to play the Love Game for real, there was Roland, all six feet four of him, getting out of his soft-top Mercedes in the Redhill car park.

I arrived at the club on the appointed day with my evening gear in a small suitcase; I would shower and change there after my workout. Keith was under the impression I was attending a girlfriend's birthday celebration, and therefore wouldn't be back till late. By now I felt terrible about the whole idea of deceiving Keith. In my confusion and guilt, his faults had become invisible; I could only see his good side. He deserved better than this: he was a caring husband, a good provider, and he tried his best – there were plenty worse than him...

After hitting ball, bending and stretching, pumping iron and total immersion in chlorinated water, my nerves were no better. Why was I doing this to myself? It was like some kind of medieval ordeal. As I finished blow-drying my hair before the changing-room mirror, I regarded my over made-up doll-like face and had a moment of acute unreality. The old Penelope Burke was about to be killed off, but the new one had yet to be born. So who was this strange individual in the glass? I didn't know, and I'm sure she didn't either.

Wearing a short white silk backless dress with frilled straps, no bra, no stockings, earrings, ankle chain and white high heels, I felt like a parody of a real person: part virgin, part life-size inflatable doll. This doll image was becoming stronger – I even experienced myself as hollow like a doll, or perhaps pumped up with compressed air. I needed to fill the void – with alcohol.

In the bar I ordered a large gin and tonic and swallowed it quickly; then I had a martini. When Roland arrived, I was lightheaded and more relaxed. He smelled of expensive aftershave and looked great in a grey-green crumpled Italian designer suit and a black jersey-style shirt, top button done up, no tie. We had fresh martinis and chatted about the time since we'd seen one another. It was so decadent, so beautifully wicked to be making small talk on the eve of such a momentous occasion.

Now I was enmeshed with Roland again, I was locked into my fantasy, on the other side of the looking glass, so to speak, instead of observing its frame with detached horror. The new Penelope Burke was flowering into life: the old P B had to go. There was simply no stopping it. Once I'd accepted this, my trepidation vanished altogether. Things probably wouldn't be as bad as I'd thought. Keith would be cut up for a while, but he'd soon find someone else – a dowdy secretary from his law firm who'd do his bidding, take instruction from the Commodore and Mrs B, become pregnant to order. It wasn't going to be me anymore – I was freeeee!!!

The June evening was warm and balmy, and Roland had the top down on the Mercedes. I plumped into the soft opulent leather seat which felt gorgeous against my bare arms and thighs. When we got out into the country, he put his foot down and I was pinned back in my seat with the slipstream lifting my hair and the trees whizzing past on either side as in a Road Runner cartoon. This was it – the new accelerated supercharged future. I was getting used to it already.

Roland's home was equal to my hopes: a large white-walled thatched cottage – probably two or three knocked into one – set in acres of secluded lawn. He led me through a panelled hallway into a lounge where old leather furniture and landscape paintings lived with a computer and fax machine. From here we entered the conservatory and went through double doors and across the back lawn to a table and two chairs set against a backdrop of mature conifers, roses and Greek statues.

Roland left me to meditate in this paradise before returning with an ice bucket, champagne and two glasses. We drank a toast, then Roland brought smoked salmon, Chinese leaves and frisée, and granary rolls. I could do hardly more than nibble at the food, for I was high as a helium-filled balloon broken free of its string. It was partly the drink, of course,

67

and also the surroundings, the atmosphere, and the marvellous trajectory events were following; but mostly it was *desire* whose juices were coursing through every vein and capillary and swirling around my stomach and loins like a whirlpool of warm cream.

A moment arrived when we weren't eating or talking, just looking into one another's eyes. Roland brushed my cheek with his forefinger, then put his hand on my bare shoulder beneath the frill of the strap. It was like a mild and very pleasurable electric shock. Our mouths met and fused, and I was back in my dream of the department store. There is no better sensation in the world, I think, than that of living a dream or a dream coming true. The fusion of our lips was the fusion of dream and actuality: for an ecstatic second, I honestly didn't know which was which.

We moved our chairs together and Roland stroked my hair between kisses and sips of champagne. After we'd finished the bottle, he took my hand and led me to the bottom of the garden where we came upon an outbuilding of rough stone blocks and no windows. Roland unlocked and opened its large double doors, then he went inside and put on an array of lighting. '*Et voilà!*' he said, and I entered this enchanting space, a technological fairyland.

Hanging from a roller near the ceiling was a large buff colorama, rich under the modelling lights of four flash heads with crinkled silver-backed umbrellas, all wired up to an impressive generator. The focus of the set was an antique chaise longue, ornately carved and covered in blue velvet. Roland had a fridge in the studio from which he produced more champagne and chilled glasses. He snapped out the overhead lights and the chaise longue took on the aura of a stage in a theatre when the performance is just about to start.

'Should I sit here?' I asked.

'Of course. Relax. Enjoy.' He poured me some champagne and placed glass and bottle on a small side table, making them part of this developing composition. I kicked off my shoes and assumed a reclining position, digging my toes into the velvet as I sipped and bubbles went up my nose. It crossed my mind that Roland was about to do it here and now, and my stomach lurched in rapturous seizure. But no, he emerged from the shadows holding a Nikon fitted with a motor drive and bulk magazine.

'That's perfect,' he said. 'Don't move.'

Quickly he repositioned the lights and attached a long cord to the camera. Then he snapped me and all four flashes popped in unison, an orgasm of light which made everything swirl in electric blue after image.

'Good. Well done. Now give me *more...*'

In response I made my position more upright and arched a shoulder towards the camera, adopting a sultry, pouting expression.

'Great!' Roland said and fired off two more shots.

What style this guy had! Imagine Keith even *conceiving* let alone constructing a setup like this as a prelude to sex. Roland was light years ahead – practically in another dimension.

'Now I want you to try something,' he said. 'Lose all inhibition. Do what you want. Let the *real you* come out of hiding.'

At last, the penny dropped! This wasn't *just* a piece of fancy foreplay – Roland was putting me through my paces, testing to find out if I had what it takes. So, my new future might also include a new *career* – as a photographic model. This exceeded even my most extravagant fantasies. I took another gulp of champagne and really *thrust* my being towards the lens, experimenting with a variety of poses and postures – arrogant profiles, thoughtful three-quarter views, the candid full face: smiling, half smiling, frowning; disdainful, superior, vulnerable; little girl, sex kitten, whore – I ran the gamut of possibilities, each click of the shutter and explosion of flash egging me on to improvise more fluently, to draw on my reserves to the utmost, to go further than ever before, to give my *all*, my everything.

It was as a natural extension of this process that I began to slide the straps of my dress off my shoulders and down my arms. Roland clicked away frenziedly, bawling messages of encouragement. After numerous bare-shoulder shots, I was left with the drooping dress cupped to my bosom, knowing that if I released my hands it would fall and I'd be naked to the waist. Logically it was the next step, and I couldn't stop or act coy now. I had to be professional. Besides, I had an overwhelming urge to reveal myself – to put that which is normally private on public view. I needed that kick, and I was ready to handle it.

I spread my arms and the dress fell; then I stood, stepped clear of it and did a sequence of new poses, some free standing, others using the couch for support. When I felt the time was right – and my sense of timing was now beautifully in synchronization with some cosmic master clock – I balanced my bottom on the edge of the cushioning, and with legs stretched forward, heels just touching the floor, I wriggled out of my panties, as slowly and deliberately and voluptuously as I knew how.

I was renewed, reborn, decisively transported into the realms of excellence. I'd done that which was absolutely forbidden – the thing that a lifetime of conditioning was supposed to prevent. At last, I had made it to membership of that elite club where you wrote your own rules and consummated your every potential. My banishment from the ordinary world which Keith and his like inhabited was complete.

Naked apart from earrings and ankle chain, I reclined on the couch in the manner of Manet's 'Olympia' – all I needed was a slave girl at my feet with a mirror. I stretched and luxuriated to give Roland a variety of poses, avoiding the obviously pornographic type. Then I thought, *Why hold anything back?* and I slid around to face the camera, spreading myself like a starfish, remaining rigid with eyes closed in a gesture of total surrender. I wondered if at last Roland would take this as the cue to shed his clothes and join in – to, as Rimbaud would say, *montrent la bite*.

But closing my eyes was a mistake, for it made me suddenly aware of the massive amount of alcohol I had drunk – way beyond my normal limits. The studio rolled like a ship in a storm; heaviness and nausea spread from stomach to head in big engulfing waves. I sat up and took notice of my naked body.

I thought, *What on earth am I doing…?*

The rest I remember only as fragments. Roland draping a dressing gown over my shoulders…me staggering around the studio and knocking over a light before falling over myself…being crouched on hands and knees on the cold stone terrace and puking into the flowerbeds. I woke up at five in the morning in a small spare bedroom. My head was still in orbit and so sore I hardly dare move it. But I had to get home fast – *and* think up a cover story to tell Keith. I wished I could die, quickly and painlessly. My dress and panties were neatly folded on a nearby chair. I put them on and reached the bathroom just in time to be sick again. Then I phoned a taxi and went home, making it into bed just before seven without waking Keith, thank goodness.

It was only later in the day, after I'd slept a great deal more and knitted my remaining brain cells back together with coffee, that I was able to reflect on the foolishness of the previous night. Already it was remote as a dream and just as incredible. Had I *really* stripped off and opened my legs to his camera? I could scarcely believe it, and only by an exercise of logic and lateral thinking could I accept it must have happened. But awful though it seemed, Roland hadn't objected. In fact, he'd loved every minute of it.

So where do we go from here? I thought.

Even then I knew things would never be the same. The dream was dashed and couldn't be restored. I found Roland's number in the book and phoned to apologise, but I kept getting his answering machine. I couldn't think of a message, and besides I was paranoid about committing my voice to tape and making a permanent record after the way Keith had been acting since my late-night stop out. A recording could be used against me in some way. There already existed a permanent record of my *naked body*!

Whenever I thought about those photographs, my head came over all hot and dizzy, and I felt like the biggest idiot who'd ever lived. At the time it never sank in that there was *film* in that camera, that my every move would be captured for posterity. I'd just thought of it all as a big laugh. Now I kept thinking: *What are they actually like? When will I get to see them? Would Roland ever show them to a third party?* It came to obsess me more than the other question which was: where did I now stand with Roland?

About a week later I managed to catch him at the club. He passed me on the way to the squash court and said, 'Hi. How's the hangover?'

'Alright now,' I said.

He didn't stop. He just carried on and commenced his game. This casual attitude hurt me more than I was prepared for. I'd paraded myself naked in front of this man, and now he just fobbed me off without acknowledging there was anything special between us.

I hung around waiting for him to finish so I could be sure I wasn't just imagining things. I felt listless, deflated, almost on the point of tears. When I spotted him going to the bar I gave it five minutes, then bit my bottom lip and followed. Gregory was there but I ignored him and spoke directly to Roland.

'Look, I'm sorry about the other night...'

'It really doesn't matter. Don't give it a second thought.'

I waited but he said no more. My forehead was heating up like a cooker plate.

'Perhaps I should take *you* out to dinner,' I said to plug the silence.

'There's really no need. Forget it. Besides I'm off to the Far East soon on a protracted assignment, so I won't be around...Another time maybe.'

'Oh...right...okay...'

The photographs! – you stupid girl. *Ask him about the photographs!*

I couldn't with Gregory listening. Roland had checkmated me, and all I could do was walk away shellshocked and go and lick my wounds.

So that was it. *Finito.* It was every bit as bad as I'd thought.

I phoned Keith to tell him I would be late, then I drove to a little spot I know and cried for half an hour.

Over the next few days, I tried to work out what had gone wrong. If Roland had been testing me, then clearly I'd failed on all counts. I was neither lover nor model material. It couldn't have been *just* because I was sick – there had to be a deeper reason for the rejection. The answer was staring me in the face, but I was too stupid to see it. I'd be hopeless as a detective.

One thing did impress itself on me as time went by: I had to get back those photographs and the negatives – and I was prepared to use clandestine means. The more I thought about it, the more imperative it became. I imagined Roland showing them to Gregory and the two having a good giggle together. The worst fear was that *Keith* would somehow get to see them – by means of a prank or a gesture of spite on someone's part – these things happen.

What took place in the studio was ephemeral; the photographs were not. Archaeologists could find them fifty thousand years hence and I'd be exhibited in a museum: genitalia of female *homo sapiens* circa late twentieth century. No. I was going get to get my hands on them first.

When I was sure Roland was away on his trip, I made my strike. I waited till after dark, then I borrowed the tool kit and broke into his studio through the small back window where he had his darkroom. My total resolve to succeed drove out the fear of being caught. Luckily the studio wasn't alarmed like the main house.

It wasn't so much like breaking into a building, more like breaking into a man's psyche. My torch beam picked out the umbrella heads, the generator, the colorama – such a sombre spectacle after the euphoria of my previous visit. A bare table stood in place of the chaise longue, which I found up against a wall. A search of drawers and shelves only revealed examples of his professional work – the compromising material had to be in the locked cabinet.

I put the crowbar between door and surround and prised

it towards me with all my strength. It took fifteen frustrating minutes before the door burst open, leaving me weak and panting, soaked in sweat. Inside were row after row of foolscap files. I took one down and found it contained tissue-paper pages of negatives, thousands of exposures, each batch with a special code of letters and numbers.

Using the torch as a light box, I discovered a charcoal-bodied woman with white lips, black teeth, a white crotch and white nipples. It might have been me except the shape of the hair was all wrong – and she was on an armchair instead of the chaise longue...I flicked through to find all the negatives were of naked or semi-naked woman. I pulled down another, and another and another – they were all the same.

At the bottom of the cabinet, I found the *albums*: repositories of the selections he'd printed up for display. Each girl was named and dated and had about twenty shots dedicated to her. The similarity between the spreads was uncanny...The amateurish attempts to achieve a model-like air...the cringe-making exhibitionism of the poses...the looks of wild excitement in their eyes when they bared their privates – we'd all trodden the same path.

So, I hadn't failed the 'test' after all. This was all he ever wanted – to capture one's *image*. I remembered feeling the day after as though the ravishment had already taken place – ravishment by a lens as seeing penis, as *recording* penis. With *hindsight* I could see his whole strategy was tailored to achieving this goal. I can always appreciate crossword clues after the answer is written in – never before.

Gingerly I thumbed through album after album till I came to the most recent, and the record of that fateful night. None of the early shots were there of course; it started with the straps dangling and dress held to my chest...*Gawd!* Who did this girl think she was? The pout was copied from Marilyn Monroe, the eyes from Elizabeth Taylor in her lush period. What got to me most was the ungainly goofiness of the way I came over. I imagined I was being so graceful and sophisticated, but the camera saw it otherwise.

Can that really be me? I thought. It was enough to make me wish for reincarnation.

I flipped the page, the dress descended and there it was – *my body*...Not bad actually – it compared well with the others. Roland might be a pervert, but he knew how to compose and light a picture. The full nudes told a different story though. There was none of the nude-as-aesthetic-object quality which partially mitigated the earlier stuff: this was the projection of pure intimacy which he'd stimulated under false pretences. To obtain such material and use it in this way was tantamount to a form of abuse.

So, what did he get out of it when he surveyed this array of breasts, bums and pubic bushes, all collated, annotated and encapsulated in plastic? Was he impotent and this was the only way he could get off? Perhaps the threat of genuine intimacy was too great to handle, so he had to freeze the critical moment then masturbate over it in the other person's absence. Then again it could be the ultimate protection against AIDS. The idea that he'd not only taken this picture, but had singled it out to be blown up the biggest ignited a state of real anger in me for the first time.

Up till then I'd merely had a semi-detached fascination with his pathology and a desire to take back what was mine; now I was going to teach this boy a lesson and remove *all* his toys. I just didn't care anymore! It was like the last time I was here and had shed my knickers in gay abandon – I could feel another impulsive act coming up. Me and my fellow exploited sisters would soon be avenged!

On my way in through the darkroom, I'd noticed a bottle marked 'negative cleaner' with a 'highly inflammable' logo on the label. I checked my exit route, then made a pile of all the albums and negative files and splashed the liquid all over this mountain of filth.

Poor Roland...it was back to square one for you, my lad. Go to the bottom of the class. As I struck a match and watched its vivid flame flare against the blackness, I saw my sexual past flash before me like a drowning woman sees her whole life. I thought:

Yes, Penelope, Debbie's words have never been truer – I've gone and found myself another class A twenty-four carat tosspot-wanker-dick-brain here!

REAL HORROR

As a writer of horror stories, I'm constantly trafficking in blood and grue, chaos and dementia; but funnily enough – or perhaps not so funnily – I find the prospect of *real* horror as icky and repulsive as the next person – perhaps more. The next person doesn't see it that way though, taking it as axiomatic that someone in my 'profession' should react with ghoulish delight towards all things macabre. So, my friends whom I meet regularly in our 'HQ', the Coronation Tap cider house in Clifton, Bristol, are forever regaling me with examples of the gory, the weird and the frightening from their own experience, seeking my approbation. True, some of it is good material and I have made use of snippets – but such is my ambivalence towards horror I'm forever scared of being confronted with something *too* palpable, if you know what I mean.

My name is Jason Carruthers – I doubt you'll have heard of me. I'm only a small press horror writer, no Stephen King or Clive Barker; but within the small world of the Clifton circle, I have something of a reputation; I'm known as a 'character'. As there are several Jasons in our set, some distinguishing means had to evolve: another Jason, also a writer, became known as 'Jason the Poet'; and by the same process I was christened 'Horror Jason'. So now whenever I walk into the pub and it's crowded, all my friends go: 'Whey hey hey! It's *Horror Jason!*' and strangers look around and ask, 'Who is he? Why is he called that?' Such is the nature of my small fame; I must admit I quite like it.

It was through this soubriquet and my literary status that I got to know a guy by the name of Lenny…a cognisance I later came to regret. Like me, Lenny is also known as a 'character', but of another kind altogether. Lenny is handsome in that specifically sharp-featured Hollywood way; he radiates the reckless damaged glamour of a James Dean or a young Marlon Brando. His hair is jet-black and straight, usually gelled and combed into a quiff. His eyes are hard and very dark. He always wears black, which contrasts appropriately with his highly pallid skin. His body is lithe and snaky, and his actual presence feels more reptilian than human. Lenny stands out vividly as a personality; once experienced his image is unforgettable; you could recognise him from hundreds of yards away.

In much that manner, I saw Lenny out and about long before I came into contact with him. People I knew fed me with information. Lenny had a reputation as a hard case; he liked to pick fights when drunk and he was a very good fighter. Apparently, he'd done time for assault or malicious wounding. Another school of thought had him down as a big-time drug dealer, or perhaps a bank and post office raider. Certainly, he always had large amounts of money on him, but never did any ordinary paid work. Someone like Lenny naturally engendered a portmanteau of myths to follow him around.

There was a period when a kind of intense staring-out and evaluation went on between him and myself in the Coronation Tap. He was coming there more frequently, having deserted the Mall, his regular haunt. He would eye me in a way which might have been sexual, and for a while I was apprehensive he might harbour those kinds of intentions; but my sources assured me he wasn't gay. Then one early evening when the bar was quiet and I was alone, sipping a slow pint of Taunton cider and scribbling in an A5 notebook, Lenny sauntered in, wearing tight black Levis, leather bomber jacket and elastic-sided winklepicker boots, his body language stylised as a dancer's. He ordered a pint, then came over and sat with me, smiling hugely, immediately intimate as though we'd been best friends for years.

'You write horror stories, don't you?' He pointed to my notebook, now closed. 'Is that one you're working on at the moment?'

'That's right,' I said brightly. 'I'm always working. I'm never not working.'

From there we launched into a fulsome, uninhibited conversation on the nature of horror, which didn't relent as the others gradually filed in, got their pints and clustered around. Lenny asked me what my stories were about, how many I'd had published, in what magazines and so forth. I was impressed by his intelligence and incisive questioning; he had a fair knowledge of the genre and had read quite extensively at its popular end – King, Herbert, Hutson, Straub. What he was most interested in, it turned out, was probing what lies behind the horror-writing process.

'What do you use as source material for your descriptions of violence and gore?' he asked me. 'Where does it come from – apart from your imagination?'

'Oh...from violent films, textbooks of forensic medicine, the odd real-life incident...' I was fairly drunk by now and had stopped feeling nervous.

'Have you ever seen anybody really badly hurt?'

'Yes, a couple of times. Once I saw a road accident victim lying in the gutter. One arm was practically torn off and twisted up behind his back, and the whole of the side of his head was ripped open, a bloody mess. He was conscious though, and I'll never forget the look in his eyes.

'Another time I saw a guy sitting in the street after a knife attack. His belly had been slashed open in three or four places – really deep wounds – and he was trying to hold it all together. Where he was cut, you could see a cross-section of the various layers of skin and subcutaneous tissue – it looked like the edge of a thick carpet with rubber underlay, and it had that same floppy quality to it too.'

Lenny smiled and nodded approvingly. I was aware that I'd put on a performance for his benefit, trying to live up to my 'Horror Jason' identity, and that we were now on the threshold of a friendship. Also, I was secretly pleased that my reserve and squeamishness had been largely in remission tonight, and I was able to discuss the topic in a forthright, even macho manner. But there was something about Lenny which made me feel uneasy on a deep, somewhat inaccessible level. I couldn't pin it down then; I just perceived a vague aura of abnormality and danger about him, coupled with the idea that opening up to him, as I'd done, was a big mistake.

I saw quite a lot of Lenny over the following months. He infiltrated my circle of friends in the pub, and sometimes latched on to the group at closing time when we went back to someone's flat to have a smoke and watch a video. When he found out where I lived, he would show up at unexpected moments and drag me off to parties, clubs or on wild stoned midnight car rides. He was almost always drunk, stoned, on coke, acid or some combination of substances. A few of my friends – Dominic and Steve in particular – said Lenny did the same to them; and Rosie and Jane, who came into the pub for a few halves and lived nearby, said he popped in now and again and shared some grass with them.

Being a writer, I naturally found Lenny an interesting type, good copy, and I studied him assiduously. But his visits and his presence in the pub got to feel invasive after a time; I needed to cool off, have some space away from him. Because of our involvement I was doing less than my normal quota of writing and it was depressing me.

I knew I could never express any of this directly to Lenny, for when I was with him, I was a changed person – I was *his* person, the person he wanted me to be. I felt like I'd been 'recruited' by him, and I had my place in his 'army' and had to follow orders and act my part properly. In short, I was frightened of his disapproval – I was something of a coward.

As well as Lenny getting to know my friends, I also gained a passing acquaintance with his. What a crew! Biker barbarians. Psychotic punks. Fascist hippies. He had the knack of picking up the weirdest people imaginable. They talked of overnight stays in locked psychiatric wards, organised punch-ups with the police at Stonehenge and other flashpoints, running dope and ecstasy from Amsterdam as if it were all the normal stuff of day-to-day life. In their company, Lenny revealed more of himself than when talking to me and my friends alone. His easy, tolerant way with matters of violence and the extreme misfortune of others was truly disconcerting, unsettling.

Where do genuine misgivings leave off and paranoia begin? Can there ever be a clearly defined boundary? In truth, is there not an overlap?

I asked myself these questions many times as I got to know Lenny more intimately. True, he was a scary guy, into heavy things; but did that mean he posed an actual threat to me and others? Try as I may to suppress it, I could feel my paranoia escalating as each new increment of his outré behaviour made its mark. One night it got the better of me completely – due largely to that great catalyst of paranoia: too much dope.

Lenny and I were visiting this flat in Hotwells, one of his favoured haunts. The guys who hung out there took no prisoners when it came to dope sessions, and there would be bongs, chillums, wedge pipes, hubble-bubble pipes, hot knives, as well as big firework joints all circulating and criss-crossing the group, so you got very stoned very quickly. On the night in question, we were smoking some killer Nepalese black, and by the time I realised I was over the top, I was already three-quarters of the way towards Venus.

My heart was thumping very hard, and I felt as though my brain was peeling itself away in layers and dissolving into a halo of gas around my head. As I looked around the room, everything took on a threatening symmetry: objects and faces appeared like chessmen lined up strategically to attack me. I was anxious to the point of wanting to escape from my skin.

Inevitably out of this state came the thoughts and images I desired least – flesh lacerating under the knife, arteries squirting like geysers, bones splintering into meaty compound fractures, nerves severed like dead telephone lines, caved-in skulls oozing their red-grey soft centres. The human body – mine in particular – seemed an intensely vulnerable item at that moment, and I was gripped by a deathly self-fuelling fear of that vulnerability being put to the test.

I glanced around at Lenny, sitting next to me on the old sofa, laughing, joking and gesticulating in ebullient exchange with the others. Unlike me, he was enjoying the high; it seemed somehow obscene. He appeared gaudy and theatrical like a clown or a Batman villain, imbued with that same *film noir*, neon-lit tinge of cartoon and comic-book menace. Soon I began to hallucinate, seeing his face in the manner of a Picasso painting with several planes visible at once, as though my vision had become five dimensional. The extra aspects had an archetypal quality, that of Greek gods or mythical heroes; but then fresh fear detonated in my stomach and the projections turned nasty...Ape-featured Neanderthals, medieval Japanese warlords, Rasputin, Hitler, distorted tribal masks, chimeras with luminous compound eyes and wings for ears, horned black-faced demons...

Next thing, my powers of rationality broke down completely in an onslaught of full-blown paranoia. I became totally convinced that Lenny was about to attack me; and moreover that it was all pre-planned and the others were in league with him – in league to enact a kind of sicko amusement for the evening with me as sacrificial lamb. I had to get out of there – it was imperative and non-negotiable. Thinking this, I was already on my feet, and I turned and charged through two doors and out into the street, not giving anyone a chance to question me and try to persuade me to stay. I'd seen other people make these spontaneous exits from dope sessions before, and now, vividly, I understood why.

Outside the night was magical, the clear autumn sky a trillion patterned points of violet and maroon interspersed with gold dust. I walked up to Clifton, coming upon the illuminated suspension bridge – a million-dollar necklace hanging in the night. From there I covered a further four miles, allowing the dope to wear off and my paranoia about Lenny to subside and take on a reasonable perspective. I realised it was silly, but on subsequent days the horripilation returned, perpetually triggered by his presence.

Try as I may, I just couldn't shake off the idea that Lenny

wanted, and intended, to attack me – and you know, it couldn't have been *all* paranoia because one night he did just that.

It was a Friday night and the whole Tap crowd were around at Dominic's place to watch the big match on his twenty-eight-inch television. Everyone was drunk; we'd started early on the Taunton in the pub, and now we were into the flagons of Natch and Thatchers, and the cans of K. Lenny didn't show up till nearly eleven, when the match was in its final stages. He came in with his mate Mickey and a three-pint bottle of Smirnoff, which they said they'd won in a raffle. The bottle was almost empty.

I was sitting in a low reclining chair in a corner of the lounge and Lenny was crouching on the carpet to one side of me. He'd been unusually quiet and was staring ahead with the smouldering, demented, almost cross-eyed expression of the terminal inebriate. Being pleasantly drunk – and unparanoid – myself, I found this rather comical and I chuckled.

'You've had a skinful tonight, haven't you, Lenny?' I said jovially.

I didn't remotely expect what happened next, nor did I believe it for several seconds afterwards. Lightning quick, Lenny darted forwards and butted me above the right eye. Even though the impact and the pain were muted by my own large alcohol intake, I was stunned by how hard a blow it was; and this was confirmed as everyone in the room turned and focussed on us.

Now furious, I stood up and drew back my fist to take a swing at Lenny; but someone – Steve – grabbed hold of it and held me back. Simultaneously Lenny squared up to me, but Dominic, Johan, Mickey and others moved to block him.

'Fancy your chances, do you?' Lenny bellowed. '– You public school *tosser!* Come on then. Let's go! LET'S GOOOOO!!!' He hopped from foot to foot and smashed his fist into his other palm as Mickey took a tighter grip on his shoulder.

'Chill out, Lenny, for fucksake,' he said.

I'd never seen anyone quite so angry – and about nothing, which made it all the more ridiculous. Lenny was the human equivalent of a rabid dog, charged with an awesome, unnatural energy. His teeth were clenched and his cheek muscles spread and contorted as though affected by huge G force. His head was vibrating like a drill bit. On reflection, I was very relieved I wouldn't have to fight him.

Dominic and Steve were steadily shunting him towards the door with cries of '*Out! Out!*' in answer to all his protestations. I think it was only Mickey's restraint which prevented him from going completely ape and taking on the lot of us.

When Lenny was finally gone Steve said, 'That guy's bad news. Bad, bad news.'

Just *how* bad remained to be seen.

I hadn't seen Rosie and Jane in the Tap for several weeks, but when I next saw them it was clear something was wrong. Rosie, normally animated and talkative, ready to give a lecture on some green or pacifist theme, was cowed and silent, her gaze fixating on the floor. And Jane, generally a happy soul, looked grave as she huddled very close to Rosie, covering one of her hands as you would a child's.

I sat down with them and chatted. Jane did all the talking and her replies were perfunctory and superficial, as if conversation was a terrific chore. They refused my offer of another drink and we'd just about dried up, when Jane said,

'What happened to your eye?'

'Huh! Lenny,' I replied. 'He nutted me. No reason...he just nutted me.'

Now she frowned and became very serious indeed. 'Look, we're going,' she said. 'Come back and have a coffee with us...'

At this Rosie tugged at Jane's hand and shook her head. Jane whispered, 'It'll be okay, love.'

Rosie and Jane. In an unkind moment, inspired by too much cider, they'd been christened 'Laurel and Hardy', and it had stuck. Rosie was Laurel: she was thin with a willowy neck, arms and legs, and Olive Oyl-like large lugubrious eyes.

Jane was Hardy: solid and wide more than fat, like a double-fronted house, with a cheerful dependable earthmother disposition. They shared a comfortable ground floor flat, often a focus for small get-togethers.

In her own territory Jane dropped her reserve further, and I could see how agitated she was as she put on the kettle and prepared the coffee cups. Also, I became aware that Rosie, sat facing away from me, was blubbering, almost inaudibly.

'So, what's going on?' I said.

'*Lenny*,' said Jane. '– The pox on all our lives, so it seems. Last Saturday, when I was away up in London staying with my mother, he wheedled his way in here and raped Rosie.'

'*Shit!*' I said. 'Shit…That was the day after he put one on me. Have you been to the police about it?'

'No. I told Rosie she ought to go, but she won't. Maybe you can persuade her –'

'*What's the fucking point?*' Rosie bawled, the first words I'd heard her speak. Now she looked at me, and the glaze of pain on her eyes was horrifying. 'He'll just say I consented, and there's nothing to show I didn't. He worked it all out; he's a very intelligent person. Intelligent and evil. What a combination…'

My system started to secrete adrenalin, as though I was under actual attack. I chose to ignore it and spoke, though my voice was unusually staccato.

'Maybe you should go to the police…regardless of the chances of gaining a conviction…Go because…because…it's better to do something rather than nothing to assert your position as a wronged person…purely for your own sake.'

'Exactly,' said Jane. 'That's what I've been trying to get her to see.'

Rosie started to cry properly now. 'I don't want to…' she sobbed. 'I can't go through with it…'

Jane held up her hands hopelessly.

Over the next hour or so, I got the whole story. Rosie met Lenny in the pub and they chatted pleasantly – Lenny is capable of huge charm and eloquence when it suits him – and Rosie felt sufficiently at ease to ask him back for a smoke.

The atmosphere was fine during the smoke, but then Lenny snaked his arm around Rosie and tried to kiss her. When she recoiled and removed his arm, he became instantaneously violent, transforming into a 'complete monster'. He grabbed Rosie around the throat with one hand and held the other out to punch her in the face; he said he'd kill her if she didn't acquiesce, and she utterly believed him.

After witnessing Lenny's performance in Dominic's flat, I had no trouble accepting this account. In fact, I could *see* it going on in my mind's eye – so vividly I felt like the victim myself.

A few days later I bumped into Lenny in the pub, and he was all smiles and bonhomie, slapping me on the back and then buying me a drink without asking if I wanted one. I wondered how I should react; I was an actor who needed direction, needed to be given his 'motivation'. Half of me wanted to refuse the drink and call Lenny a bastard to his face; but I could already feel this half losing the struggle. I would act towards him as I'd always done, though perhaps with some minor element of standoffishness as a concession to my true feelings.

'How's the eye?' Lenny said and chuckled.

'It's been better...' I said as sardonically as I could muster.

He then started to talk about Miami, which he'd just visited, praising it as a great and wild city. No reason was given for the short visit, but I suspected a little cocaine dealing was behind it all; Lenny's conversation was smooth and voluble – a sure sign he was on coke himself.

I found myself asking questions, the writer in me stimulated and hungry for information. How could I just dismiss what he'd done to Rosie and carry on as normal? I wished I knew. I felt how a senator in the court of Caligula must have felt – secretly disgusted but just unable to display the emotion.

Somehow, we got on to the subject of violence, and Lenny gave a self-satisfied account of how he'd given 'a good kicking' to some guy who'd messed up a deal they were involved in together. My anger surfaced at this point and I was able to challenge him in the safer area of a case in which I wasn't personally involved. But it was Rosie I was thinking of.

'How can you justify that...' I began, 'injuring somebody merely because he was incompetent?'

'You *gotta* keep people in line – and show others what they'll get if they fuck you around. It's all about power; everything comes down to that in the final analysis.'

'But it's about something else too, isn't it Lenny? I think you actually *enjoy* beating up on people – I think it's your *hobby*...'

He eyed me sharply, and with unconcealed pleasure. I saw that far from annoying him, I'd impressed him.

'Well...you'd know about that too, wouldn't you?'

'What d'you mean?'

'You write horror – you do on paper what I do in real life.'

'Not at all...' I said, suddenly very nervous as though I'd started to cross a field and then discovered there was a bull in it. 'Fictional horror is not the precursor of *real* horror; it's an extension of fantasy; it's fairy tales for grownups...'

Lenny smiled and put his face close to mine. 'But isn't real horror also an extension of fantasy – the fantasy of doing it come true...?'

I had to think about this carefully. 'In some ways perhaps,' I said, 'but the *intention* is different. In one the intention is to create a work of art, to promote thought and debate; in the other the intention is to inflict actual pain, actual cruelty. How can they be the same?'

'They're more similar than you want to believe.'

'I don't buy that.'

'Of course you don't buy it. If you did, it would show you in a bad light, and you want to think of yourself as a cultured and refined man – who just *happens* to be obsessed with horror.'

'So, what are you saying? I'm really just a closet sadist?'

'You're a *potential* sadist, yes. Everybody is.'

'We're all killers and rapists underneath – you really believe that?'

'If the circumstances are right, yes. When the *playacting* at being civilized is stripped away – by a breakdown in the social order or war, for example – these things surface. Mild-mannered banks clerks get given weapons and they become homicidal beasts – history proves it.'

'History has saints as well as killers.'

Lenny grinned. 'But it's the killers who are the interesting ones...'

'You have a worrying perspective on things, Lenny,' I said.

'It worries you, I know.'

He winked at me.

A week later Rosie was dead. She slipped out of the flat early in the morning when Jane was asleep and jumped off the Clifton Suspension Bridge. When we heard, we all went around to the flat to lend support, and it was like the aftermath of those disasters you see on the TV news – the place was full of distressed, mourning relatives, and the atmosphere was cloying and claustrophobic.

When I got Jane to myself, she told me between bouts of tears what had transpired.

'Poor Rosie...I feared she wasn't going to make it, and I was right...She could see his face whenever she closed her eyes; she felt he was hiding in the flat, was watching her all the time...She said she was dammed, and couldn't face going on. I tried to get her to get help, see a councillor or something; but she was too far gone. The poor love...'

The next day there was an ugly scene. We got Jane into the pub at lunchtime to have a drink and unwind a little, and Lenny was there. Normally he never came in lunchtimes, but the tide of luck was running firmly against us. When Jane saw him, she tensed up and marched his way; we grabbed her but she shrugged us off forcefully.

'*Bastard!*' she hissed. 'Have you any idea of the trouble you've caused to how many people?'

Lenny didn't reply. He just stared her out calmly while sipping his drink and drawing on his Marlboro.

'Is that it?' he said eventually, almost bored.

Jane stamped the floor and hit her sides with her fists.

'You...you...There's no getting through to you. You're sub-human, disgusting...What do we do with people like you...?'

As we clustered closer to Jane and tried to pull her away, Lenny began to laugh.

'Take no notice, Jane,' Dominic said, and it was the wrong thing for it made Lenny laugh harder.

'Look at you all!' Lenny said. 'Who do you think you are – the fucking Spanish Inquisition? Ha, ha, ha, ha, ha...'

Soon Lenny was paralytic with laughter, holding on to the bar as his body rocked and convulsed. Jane just watched him, and the more she watched the worse the laughing jag became. There *was* something truly disgusting and obscene about his personality: Lenny was a psychopath. If I'd had any slight doubts before, this episode wiped them away.

In truth this whole Lenny business had affected me badly. I came to the uneasy conclusion that I was absorbing his ma-levolent effect by a process of slow osmosis, and soon I would be saturated. Certain 'symptoms' were clearly identifi-able.

Dating from the time of the Hotwells dope session, I'd developed an unnatural fear – a phobia almost – of physical injury. The presence of kitchen knives made me extra twitchy; I drove my car with too much caution while visu-alising accidents; violence on film or TV made me nauseous. To cap it off, my writing had suffered a major collapse: the prospect of tackling any material containing a macabre element seemed dangerous, tempting fate some-how; and that was my stock-in-trade. Some psychological protective layer had been peeled away, rendering me super-sensitive to any unpleasant stimuli. I was suffering, and I blamed Lenny.

At the root of the problem was my own compliance with Lenny. I felt I couldn't go on pretending to be his friend when I found him morally reprehensible, beyond the pale. I had to get to the end of this somehow, even at the risk of him turning against me.

What actually happened was things came to a head of their own accord.

Late next Friday night I bumped into Lenny in the Royal Oak. I'd gone there specifically to *avoid* him, but I hadn't accounted for Sod's Law. He was glad to see me, genuinely friendly, but I was way past being seduced by all that. Gradually I mustered my courage and looked him straight in the eye.

'Rosie's dead. Doesn't that mean anything to you?'

The warmth and camaraderie instantly drained from his demeanour.

'What's it supposed to mean? Shit happens, you know.'

'Is that the best you can do – "shit happens" –? You *caused* the shit, Lenny.'

His mouth turned down at the corners and his face became rigid.

'Don't push your luck, Jason. Don't get out of your depth...'

I said nothing and neither did he. We resumed sipping our drinks, and Lenny lit up his last Marlboro, crushing the empty packet to nothing with a single contraction of his hand.

'Let's go somewhere else,' he said when we'd drunk up. 'I don't like this pub.'

On the way out, someone bumped into Lenny's shoulder, and with spontaneous alacrity Lenny elbowed him sharply in the ribs.

'*Hey, steady on!*' the guy cried out in pain.

'Watch where you're going, fucker!'

Out in the dark street Lenny's anger continued to boil. He started kicking a litter bin, shouting 'fuck' over and over. I could tell he didn't want to turn his anger on me because he liked me; he didn't have that many 'real' friends and I suppose I'd become special. I could have liked him too if he wasn't so blackhearted; I may have sympathised with him if it wasn't for Rosie.

'Look,' he said, coming close to me, 'let's enjoy ourselves, okay? Let's have a good time...'

'Sure, Lenny,' I said, concluding that pacifying him was the least worse option available to me.

'Good. We'll try that new club on Park Row.'

It was loud, smoky and heaving with bodies, pushing up against one another in complex ebbing and flowing tides – the sort of place I hate. We settled in a corner of the back bar, and Lenny set about getting purposefully smashed, whacking back vodka, tequila and Jack Daniels with Stella Artois chasers. The drunker he became, the more his attempts at friendliness, at having 'a good time', came to resemble a hideous parody of those things – a third-rate clown act that wasn't convincing. He wasn't having – couldn't have – a good time: the guy was sick.

And Lenny wasn't the only drunk at the bar. A big, thuggish, bullet-headed guy of around six feet three and twenty stone was goofing around, blabbering to people at random. He was so drunk he couldn't remember he'd talked to us only minutes earlier, and repeated the exact same story in an almost incomprehensible treacly slur. He'd just been discharged from the army, and was now about to embark on a career as a timeshare salesman on the Costa Del Sol. He would be the best timeshare salesman there ever was in the history of timeshare selling. I kept trying to edge away, but he kept blocking off any exit space with his bulk.

Eventually I managed to slip out for a piss, and when I returned the guy was still going on at Lenny in that pointless argumentative way that drunks do. I was about to reach for my pint when the guy picked it up first and brought it to his lips.

'Hey mate, that's my drink,' I said, tapping him on the shoulder.

He turned towards me with a kind of braindead malicious stare.

'This is *my* drink,' he said, pointing at it.

'No, it's mine. I'm certain of it.'

'I said it's *mine!*' He lashed out at my shoulder with a beefy paw, and I staggered backwards.

The sharp unexpected contact was appalling, and now violence was right at the top of the agenda – the guy looked set to have another go, escalate things. Suddenly I was terrified,

overwhelmed by utter cowardice, ready to make any concession to stop him from hurting me. I felt weak and wobbly
and helpless. This wasn't like violence on paper which I could
control and shape to a purpose; no one was 'authoring' these
events; anything might happen from this point onwards. I
resolved that if he came at me again, I'd run to the toilets and
try to shut the door on him.

'You wanta make sumthin' of it?' he was saying over these
thoughts.

Several people were watching us by now.

'No, no,' I said. 'You keep it.'

'Keep it? It's my fuckin' drink! Al-wight? *Say* it's my fuckin'
drink...Go-awn. Say it.'

'Now look...'

'– It's *his* drink,' Lenny interjected, standing up. 'It's his
drink, not yours – you big fat gorilla. Why don't you get back
to the fucking zoo with all the other animals...?'

The guy grunted and took a swipe at Lenny; but Lenny was
already crouching away from his reach, and in the same
movement he delivered an uppercut right into the guy's
groin.

As the guy crumpled, Lenny conjured up a bottle – a Newcastle Brown bottle – and with a flick of the wrist he chipped
off the bottom on the edge of a fruit machine. His move-
ments were so fast, so sinuous, it was like watching some
superefficient stripped-down engine in action: his arm was
the con rod, the bottle the piston, driving into the guy's face,
rotating, slashing – all in a blurred seamless frenzy.

I didn't want to look at the result of this work, but I felt I
had to: it was my 'duty'; how could I miss out on this great
'opportunity' to gain such 'excellent' material?

The guy no longer had anything which you could call a
mouth; his cheek flesh was gashed right away, giving a wrap-
around view of his teeth, rendering the sense of the skull
beneath the tissue very strongly. His lower lip hung off like a
red earthworm, and one eye was punctured and leaking like
a gel sachet, while the other was closed up and oozing red
like a plum. His nose was partially detached at the root, and

the bony apertures beneath just visible. It looked like a joke-shop nose which wasn't stuck on properly, and I had to tell myself it was real...yes, this was a real face...But seeing it reduced to its component parts gave it the air of a model, of a kit you assemble – or disassemble. Real people are made this way, and this could be done to *any* of us...

I tried to suppress this perception, but already a monstrous internal pressure was chasing it, an insane mixture of anger and fear, pushing me towards hysteria. With successive violent throbs my heart jacked me up to the heights of some dire precipice from which I was now destined to fall. I held on at the edge, teetering, swaying in and out of the void.

Everyone was focussed on Lenny, still holding the blood-coated bottle. They all stood stock still like characters in a tableau vivant, no one daring to do anything to attract the attention of this maniac. But it was to me he turned, waving the bottle in the direction of the slumped, bloodied figure.

'Good one, eh, Jason?' he gasped, then laughed crazily. '*Put that in a fucking story!*'

The idea that I should 'appreciate' this deed, or, worse, that on some level Lenny had done it with the sense of my complicity, finally made my stomach heave, and that sickening combination of beer and bile gushed up into my mouth; but I managed to swallow most of it back, letting out only a little dribble.

However, Lenny zeroed-in on this and guffawed.

'Look at him!' he shouted to everybody. '– The "horror writer"! *Ha! Ha! Ha! Ha! Ha!*

Immediately I felt a second heave, a much stronger one, and I knew this time there was no way I was going to keep it down.

WHITEOUT

1.

The snow came on the afternoon of their third day, funnelling towards them across the high mountain passes in a flotilla of beige-grey nimbi, like a slow-motion explosion. As it got closer, it took the form of a giant shroud enveloping nearby pistes in ghostliness, its multiple arms stretching wider and even creeping up from behind. Soon individual flakes could be decoded within the milky down drop, and then there was the magic of six-pointed stars appearing on the bright Gore-Tex of their ski suits, sparking off Christmassy, snow-romp nostalgia.

Rod lifted his grey-lens goggles and smiled at the smiling Caroline, who wore a dark cowl and sunglasses like some exotic designer nun.

'Whey hey! hey!' he yelped. 'It's here. *At laaasst!!!*'

'Thank goodness...'

'We're cured –'

'Saved.'

Rod looked around, pulling the goggles back into position. All distinguishing landscape features were disappearing in the swirling rhythms of the storm; suddenly they were alone in alien space.

'Come on,' he said. 'We'd better get down.'

Simultaneously they pushed off with their poles and glided through the fresh powder, already deep enough to bury their skis from sight.

'I can't see a fucking thing!' Caroline exclaimed between giggles.

Rod laughed and reflected that he felt happy. Caroline disapproved of the word 'fucking', and her use of it served to emphasise the unusual playfulness of the situation. This was the first moment of pure fun in a holiday which had so far been strained and difficult.

Caroline was only a few feet ahead of Rod, and yet she was hardly *there* at all – just a few charcoal streaks in the whiteness. As Rod concentrated more on this phenomenon of blanket whiteness, it took him over mesmerically. He'd skied in blizzards before, but this was the first time he'd experienced what was becoming a total whiteout, and the effect was remarkable and quite unparalleled. He could see nothing – absolutely nothing – no shape nor definition to the surface he was skiing upon, no differentiation between ground and air, nothing at all except...

White, pure white, brilliant white, whiter than white, the whitest white you could ever imagine...His mind searched for more imagery to convey the sensation...Cottonwool white, cloud white, caster-sugar white; powdery, fluffy, duck-downy white; total white, maximum white, ultimate white...the white to end all whites...

Never had whiteness seemed so significant, so metaphysically awesome. It became the harbinger of some primal domain, the place before and after creation, a netherworld made palpable by *exclusion*, by the banishment of all the components which make up this world. People usually attributed these things to blackness, naturally, as blackness was common and this experience was not. To know true white, Rod thought, is to...is to...

He came back to himself and immediately felt fear. Caroline was lost to him in the whiteness, and the dazzling powder was drifting, reaching up to mid-calf level in places. The fear notched up rapidly towards panic as he conjectured Caroline gone off course somewhere and fallen; or worse, she could have missed the piste markers and gone over an edge.

'Caroline!' he called. Then louder, 'Caroline...! *Caroline...!!!*'

There was no reply, but Rod felt the gradient beneath him suddenly dive, requiring him to sharpen up his skiing. He did four awkward, heavy turns, then descended below a threshold where the falling snow was less dense and there was a modicum of distance perception. He could now make out the partially scribbled-in backs of other skiers, no more than floating phantom presences, but they instantly relieved him of the unnerving sense of unreality and isolation. A single skier was stopped on a hillock, looking back, and as Rod got closer he recognised the purple and royal blue of Caroline's overall.

'Shit!' he said, gooey with the relief of danger now past. 'That was hairy!'

'Wasn't it! I couldn't tell where I was going; I looked around for you and crossed my skis and nearly fell over; I just knew I had to keep going and not stop or else...'

'Phew...! Let's go and get a brandy in L'Ourson Blanc. We deserve it.'

'You like that bar, don't you?'

2.

They made do with a brandy and a coffee at the lift station bar, and deferred going to L'Ourson Blanc, their 'local', till mid-evening. In the meantime, they showered and changed in their chalet. While Caroline did her makeup, Rod performed sit-ups, press-ups, stretches and bends, grumbling that there wasn't a Nautilus machine in the chalet for him to use, and there should be with the prices they were paying.

Before their showers Rod had made a pass at Caroline, wrestling her down onto the bed with his powerful arms, grinning bright-eyed; but she'd felt too tired and had told him to wait till later. Now, as always, he was a little morose because of what he construed as a rejection. It was silly, Caroline thought.

She glanced up from her makeup mirror towards Rod, who was preening himself in front of the long mirror, inflating his chest and tensing every muscle, admiring his Rutger Hauer-from-*Bladerunner* image: the hair short, blond and scalp-hugging, its tips highlighted and roots dark; the stare hard and moody; the eyes ice-blue and armour piercing. She hoped he wouldn't keep the grudge going all evening.

L'Ourson Blanc was unusually crowded as tonight was Karaoke night. Moreover, everyone was extra ebullient because it had been snowing continuously for over five hours now, and tomorrow promised to be a brilliant day on the slopes. Caroline and Rod were sat with a group of five or six others from their chalet, an unremarkable mix of people with whom they'd contracted the easily acquired, disposable friendships peculiar to skiing holidays. Norman, a plump fortyish car salesman from East Grinstead, was getting in the next round and joking that it was worth paying the high bar prices in order to be served by the lovely dusky Sabine. His wife Marjorie was thumping him on the thigh in a mock show of indignation.

Caroline felt detached from the party atmosphere. She didn't want to drink much and the fug of smoke was making her cough. Another irritation was the loud jukebox, churning out its constant stream of Euro-noise – hits old and new, where Serge Gainsborough, Cat Stevens, the Beatles, and Abba merged with the Police, Tubeway Army, Madonna and Michael Jackson. After several nights such as this, Caroline would have preferred to stay in and read, or even watch French TV; but Rod was insistent they had to go out and 'enjoy' themselves.

When Rod had swallowed the last of his new lager, she'd hardly touched hers, and refused his offer of another. He took orders from the group and Caroline watched him as he approached the bar, sidling automatically to the place where Sabine was serving. She made a big show of recognising Rod, jutting out her chin and pouting at him with her pneumatic damson lips. They talked for some time before she took his order, and Caroline strained to see around the heads of other customers, glimpsing flashes of Sabine's big-toothed smiles and gesticulating long-nailed fingers.

Caroline felt a swell of anger, and for a microsecond actually considered getting up and walking out. Perhaps she was overreacting, but the attitude of tarts like Sabine was really hard to take. To men they were the personification of loquacious charm, grace and helpfulness; but to women – particularly other attractive women – they displayed a contempt which bordered on catlike hostility. On their first evening here, Caroline had addressed Sabine pleasantly and in French, which she spoke well, only to receive a curt reply in English, as if to say: you're a stupid tourist and you'll be treated as such. Ever since then Sabine had reserved a special dark scowl of projected malice for whenever she saw Caroline, and Caroline hated her for this senseless and unnecessary posturing.

Sometime later, Sabine came out from behind the bar to collect glasses, undulating languidly from table to table while the men tracked her with robotic eyes. There was always one which the men all gawped at, and in L'Ourson Blanc it was Sabine. She had the deep olive sheen, dark animal eyes and ringleted black hair of the standard Hollywood belly dancer, and she acted this dreadful female stereotype with maximum relish. Everything she wore was artfully skin-tight: a black Lycra body, black leggings, imitation snakeskin knee boots and a four-inch-wide black patent leather belt with fake leopard-skin trimming on the loop. To Caroline, the overdone curves of her ass and her big heavy breasts matched for cheapness her gaudy goth makeup and profusion of junk bangles and rings. On the plus side, she was tall and had a small waist; but out of a bra those breasts would be pendulous and probably have stretch marks. She wasn't near as perfect as men liked to believe.

When Sabine came closer Caroline transferred her gaze to Rod, and saw him monitoring her progress with an expression of drunken simpleminded approval. This wouldn't be the first time she'd had to warn him.

'Stop looking at her, Rod.'

'Uh...? I'm not looking *at* her; I'm looking generally. She just happens to be in my field of vision.'

'You *are* looking at her.' The anger was swelling again.

'Don't be stupid.'

'Rod...?'

'Look, Caroline. Stay cool. You're going to ruin the evening.'

At that moment there was a husky amplified breath, and a young man in a red bow tie announced the Karaoke was about to commence.

3.

Sat on the bed with Caroline, Rod felt the pleasant sea roll of intoxication take him up higher, and he ran his fingers through her silky chestnut hair, stroking an ear with his thumb.

'Do you feel *in the mood* now?' he said in as gentle a tone as he could muster.

Caroline exhaled disinterestedly, and her body crumpled. 'I'm whacked, Rod. Really.'

'You said "later" – it's later now.'

'I just want to go to sleep.'

'We are on holiday, you know...'

'Yes, Rod – a *skiing* holiday in case you haven't noticed. I've had all the exercise I can manage for one day, and there's a strenuous day ahead of us tomorrow. Aren't you tired?'

'No. I've got plenty of spare energy.'

'Go and have a wank or something.'

'Charming...'

Later, when they were lying in bed together in the darkness, Caroline cocooned in her thick winceyette pyjamas and bed socks, Rod felt they could be a retired couple in their sixties for all the vibrancy that existed between them. They'd been together five and a half years now, three of them married. He was twenty-nine and she thirty-one.

Is this what it's going to be like for the next forty years? he thought. Excuse after excuse?

Their ingenuity was sometimes remarkable, amusing even; but the chain they formed always spelled out the same message: he was doomed to a moribund sex life. In their first year together, they used to do it in fields, do it in caves; they did it spontaneously – and frequently. Why not now? That stuff Rod sometimes read in Caroline's magazines about couples going off sex after a few years wasn't nonsense; it merely seemed like that written down on glossy paper in a cringe-making style; in actual fact it was a true and very real syndrome.

Unable to quieten down, Rod's mind instead shifted gear,

and he found himself back in L'Ourson Blanc, studying Sabine's black-clad form moving sinuously through space like a cobra to pipe music. He considered the acreage of her cleavage, its rise and fall, its smooth texture, like polished antique pine, the prominence of the clavicles, the ample nipple-imprinting breasts...He smiled and felt wicked. Then he conjectured a might-have-been scenario: suppose he were a bachelor, or Caroline had died, or he was simply here on his own...He knew Sabine would go for it – she was obviously the type.

Rod fully felt the limitlessness of his male potentiality; he could take on a thousand Sabines right now, so it seemed. He glanced over at Caroline, breathing rhythmically, fast asleep, and wondered for how long they could continue maintaining this stagnant status quo.

4.

After hearing the muffled, warlike booms of the avalanche cannons overlaying her dreams, Caroline woke at seven to find Rod already up, and brilliant sunlight flooding the room. Blinking herself into alertness, she joined him at the window and there they witnessed the world reborn in white perfection. The village below them sparkled with unreal Winter Wonderland quaintness, its roofs, hedges and verges like thickly iced cake decorations. Beyond it lay the flawless white topography of the slopes, the tiny distant bug-like forms of the piste-bashers rendering its surfaces supreme.

Getting ready to go out, they put on so much total sunblock that they resembled mime artists, and Rod started acting the part, feeling along imaginary surfaces to Caroline's trumpeting giggles. She was so relieved last night's bad vibrations had properly gone, seemingly lasered away by the luminosity of the morning.

Ascending in the big fast gondola to the top station, they had an evolving panorama of the many rolling pistes which made up the large ski area, gleamingly bright almost to the point of pain even through sunglasses. Skiers at various distances seemed respectively like tiny flecks of dust, like swarming ants, like toy soldiers, like Action Man dolls, like the Little People. When Caroline and Rod alighted at the dazzling yet refrigerated summit, it was like landing on another planet, a better or idealized version of Earth, the sartorial trappings of skiing – zippered suits, heavy boots, reflective eyewear, showy headgear – perfectly complementing the illusion.

Twinkly, glittery, scintillating snow, a trillion diamond points of kiln-baked crust, of contoured Styrofoam sculpture, lay at their feet. Rod pointed out the direction of his planned route, and they pushed off and glissaded with such frictionless beauty it was like travelling through the nap of some incredible white velvet. As the incline steepened, Caroline did a quick zigzag formation of majestic turns, the new snow making her twice the skier she really was. Rod had bombed on ahead in his usual way, giving a performance of technique to an audience which existed more in his own mind than anywhere, Caroline reckoned.

Rod's route took them right over to the far side of the mountain, then along a boulevard run through a forest of pencil-straight pines to connect up with the next mountain's lift system. Here they discovered vast new uplands of long, undemanding blue and red runs, which Caroline favoured, and they did two full circuits to take them up to their lunch at a lavish and expensive Swiss-style restaurant.

In the afternoon Rod, primed by strong lager, led them further and higher, right into the far corner of the ski area. They spent about half an hour ascending a series of long drag lifts when Caroline became apprehensive about where they were headed. She had told Rod 'No blacks', and on their second day had refused to take the cable car to the top of the infamous 'Death Valley' black; now she suspected they were approaching this same black run, but from the other side of the mountain. A look at her piste map at the top confirmed this was true, and she skied after the retreating Rod, catching up with him just as the ominous steep face of the run proper came into sight around a curve.

'You've tricked me,' Caroline said. 'You knew I didn't want to go down here.' Her breath was coming fast, issuing gouts of condensation into the shaded cold.

'It'll be okay,' Rod droned. 'The run's in beautiful condition with the new snow. Just take it at your own pace.'

'I don't want to! – And you can't make me.' Caroline was really tensing up now; the day's enchanted atmosphere had been snatched away and they were right back in familiar sword-clash mode.

Rod made a blubbering sound through his lips. 'Look. You've got to stretch yourself sometimes, Caroline. Otherwise, you might as well be in your bathchair already.'

'I've told you before. I don't believe in taking risks.'

'But it isn't a foolhardy risk. You know you can do it – you're just really testing out the power of your own will. It's not like deliberately putting yourself in danger for the sake of it.'

'I don't care how you rationalise it, Rod. If you end up *in a cast* it doesn't matter what you thought you were doing to get there. The bones won't heal any faster.'

'But if you hold the knowledge of your own supremacy in your mind, you can't go wrong. You'll sail down, like Jesus walking on the water.'

'Rubbish!'

'Don't be like that...Come on...'

'No! I'm not bloody coming!' Her voice was grating and ugly with anger now; she was shocking herself with its intensity, and at the same time hating Rod for bringing it out in her. 'Why you have to ruin everything by pulling stunts like this, I don't know...I'm going to walk back up and take the cable car down. I'll meet you at the bottom...'

'That's stupid.'

'Fuck off, Rod.' She was already unclipping her boots from her bindings. Before Rod could frame his next argument, she'd picked up her skis and began the long uphill trudge to the cable car station.

The climb did Caroline good, helped her get the quarrel into perspective. At the beginning of the holiday, she'd wanted to go into ski school for the mornings, but Rod had groaned at the prospect; so they'd made a deal to ski together providing they avoided difficult and arduous terrain. Now Rod had reneged on their deal, employing calculated deviousness in order to do so. It was yet another example of the way he tried to control and mould her against her will, and she wasn't having it. Now feeling fully justified, she resolved to book herself some private lessons for the final two mornings of the holiday, the moment they got back down to the village.

5.

Rod lingered at the breakfast table, fidgeting with a bread roll he didn't want to eat and listening to the chalet girl washing up in the kitchen. It was after half past nine and everyone had gone, including Caroline to her lesson. Now he could go ski anywhere he wanted without opposition, he was totally unmotivated by the prospect. He had a twinge of a hangover from the gut-rot wine he'd drank the night before, and in addition felt bored and oppressed by the ongoing war of wills with Caroline.

He got his jacket and gloves and went for a wander in the village. There was weak sunshine, and partially melting snow was lumped high on roadside verges like a congress of failed snowmen. He went into a newsagent and surveyed the array of souvenirs, soft toys, risqué postcards of girls with bare suntanned bums high in the mountains. Picking up a copy of the *Daily Express*, he connected briefly with the latest woes of the Major government, then dropped the paper, not wishing the normality of British life to intrude on him here.

This is stupid...he said to himself. He resolved to go back and get changed, then map out a little circuit he could complete before meeting Caroline for lunch.

Approaching the steps of his chalet, he saw the tall wild-haired form of Sabine sauntering towards him. She had an armful of giant baguettes, and she wore a short dress with bare legs despite the cold. The instant Rod saw her, it was like a flare gun had been fired in his stomach. Automatically he raised a hand and waved, and she jiggled her free hand back at him in that extra-friendly continental way. He waited at the gate for her to reach speaking distance, then they exchanged deeply expressive 'Hellos'.

'I didn't see you last night,' Sabine said in her husky, syrup-thick voice.

'No. We stayed in and played a game. You had to write down the name of a famous person, then swap it with somebody else, then stick it on your forehead without looking and ask questions to guess who it is. It went on for about five hours.'

'Your English games...' She shook her head and smiled, manipulating her full wide mouth in a way which Rod felt magnetically. 'Are you going skiing?'

'Thinking about it.'

'You're not sure?'

'I will go eventually. I'm just being a bit lazy.'

'Where's your wife?'

'She's having a private lesson.'

Sabine chirped with laughter, and Rod spontaneously joined in. The sun suddenly seemed a lot warmer.

'That sometimes means something else...' Sabine explained.

'A euphemism...' said Rod.

'Comment? A *yoof*–?' She frowned, crinkling her nose.

'Doesn't matter.' Rod shook his head.

There was a silence during which Rod looked coolly into Sabine's huge chocolate eyes, feeling that pull again. She returned the stare measure for measure, unflinching, showing him she didn't have to hurry away with her baguettes – that *he* was her agenda of the moment. His heart began to beat faster, and then faster still. As the words started to form on his lips, he could feel the beat thumping throughout his entire frame.

'Do you want to come inside? Have a drink or something?'

'Sure.'

She was unsurprised, totally within her operational capacity here as she ambled in and dumped her burden on the dining table.

Rod felt a further rush of adrenalin as he saw there were no more barriers – the chalet girl had finished and gone; the place was empty; Caroline was occupied – and if he reached out to Sabine now, that would be it: they would end up having sex. It had happened so quickly – too quickly – but if he didn't take the chance now it would evaporate; the perfect architecture of the moment would be lost.

Sabine had her arms folded and was watching him, waiting for him to do something.

'What would you like to drink?' Rod said, immediately feeling foolish at employing a delaying tactic.

'I don't want a drink.' Sabine was not smiling now.

After a brief pause, she came up to where he was standing and looked closely into his face, a divinator reading the runes. He felt the magnetic tug more profoundly than ever now, and with it a sense of Sabine's complete mastery as an erotic player. By his inaction he'd been humbled, like a gambler who'd upped the stakes too far and was about to be caught out bluffing.

But when Sabine had lingered long enough for him to tune into the musky miasma of her flesh, forward motion was somehow achieved – a clicking into place of pheromonal tumblers on that primal level which overrides all intellectual processes.

Rod leant forward and they merged and kissed. Sabine was almost the same height as him, an inch short of his six feet, so he could kiss her standing without bending down. That was the first difference. The second was the way she kissed, utterly unlike Caroline. She clamped her lips tight to his with almost aggressive pressure while her vigorous tongue darted and rotated deep into his mouth. The novelty of kissing like this made his head pound with excitement; it evoked teenage responses he thought were gone forever. He ran his hands up her back and felt the muscle-tone solid beneath tight skin, and then around to her breasts pressing against him, so

105

definite a *statement* in every way. Yes, Sabine was absolutely different to Caroline in ways he could never have precisely foretold.

She broke off just as his enjoyment was really accelerating and suggested they go somewhere more private. After quick calculation, he led her up to the green-tiled space of the second-floor bathroom, where she undressed quickly, kicking off après boots, shrugging herself free of her dress and peeling off black lace panties. Watching, Rod was zapped by the immediacy of her huge plum-dark nipples and her thick, very black pubic hair, shiny like fine electrical wiring. He hadn't seen a naked woman apart from Caroline in six years, and the image printed itself on his consciousness with branding-iron force. It was *real* – not a photograph, nor a video, but unmediated actuality. Black edges formed on his vision, pulsing in sync with his furious heartbeat.

Sabine opened her purse, took out a condom and tossed it to Rod. 'Come on. Get undressed. I haven't much time.'

Sensing his trepidation, she went to help him, pulling up his polo neck sweater and running long apricot-painted nails over his stomach and pectorals. 'Mmmnn...good body,' she said, and Rod went delirious with pride, feeling so glad he was committed to working-out properly. He hauled off the sweater and the rest of his clothes, thinking: It's finally going to happen. And from there it was easy to make the step to: It's *meant* to happen. As he and Sabine embraced and knelt together on the tiles, Rod was sure that Fate or some higher power had approved all of this – the circumstances were so fortuitous – and thus comforted, the fear in his stomach parcelled itself up small and melted away.

6.

Caroline was pleased when twelve o'clock came, and her second and last lesson with Gaston concluded. She had improved doubtless; her turning was tighter and more fluid due to the instruction; but the flirty innuendos of this overweight fifty-year-old were something she could have done without. Tomorrow she and Rod would be driving up through France and catching an evening ferry at Port de Calais. Another skiing holiday over. This one had seemed like an ordeal, and she wasn't at all sorry to see the whole thing pass into history.

It had been overcast and misty all morning, and now veils of snowflakes filled the air in the apron of piste by the village centre. Caroline was due to meet Rod in an hour, up at their usual mountain restaurant, and she didn't feel like more skiing in the meantime. So instead, she parked her skis outside the shopping mall and clumped in her ski boots to a little cafe she knew, which served superb hot chocolate.

Sitting down, Caroline recognised the manageress of L'Ourson Blanc two tables away, talking to another woman. Caroline sipped her drink and listened to the rat-tat-tat of their French conversation, managing to catch and decipher about three words out of five. They were discussing someone called Jacques. He was angry and exasperated about some matter, and had been issuing loud threats. Caroline heard the word 'murder'. Then she heard the name 'Sabine'. She was involved in some way...Ah ha...Sabine was Jacques's girlfriend; she had been making an idiot out of him...other men were involved. Caroline felt a smile spread on her face.

Then in a plangent voice which Caroline could easily hear and translate, the manageress said: '*That Sabine – she's a terror! And she doesn't care who knows it. On Tuesday night she had all three of the long-haired Italians in Chalet Nicole, one after the other. And only yesterday morning she had the blond Englishman in Chalet Bertrand while his wife was having a private lesson!*'

Caroline received the words, but their meaning lay in suspension for a couple of seconds, then it hit her. Then it went away again. It had to be a mistake – or some kind of elaborate joke – but it was February not April the first. She went through it again, a dreadful palpitating nervousness building inside her. Rod was the only blond Englishman in Chalet Bertrand...apart from Steven. But Steven wasn't here with his wife...It had to be Rod...But yesterday, during the private lesson? How had they fixed it up? It was too incredible...

And yet it had to be true, Caroline accepted with a worsening of her nervous state. Everything fitted in. There was Rod's strange sheepishness throughout yesterday afternoon and evening. His good behaviour had bordered on the unreal. And he'd not wanted to join the others in L'Ourson Blanc after their dinner-for-two in the next village (due to it being the chalet girl's night off). And finally, he'd shown no interest in sex on an evening when she herself wouldn't have minded. That was totally unlike Rod.

She tried to picture it: Rod and Sabine. He'd always had a cretinous streak which would make him vulnerable to the wiles of a painted-up scrubber like her...God, I wonder if he used a condom? Caroline thought. And that thought cannoned back on her, bringing home palpably the full impact of what had happened. It tore through her mind like a berserk chainsaw, stripping all composure, releasing a crazed gargantuan rage.

It was preposterous that he could go so far! The total bastard!...Caroline had to get out of the cafe. Any moment now she would start to howl like a coyote. She stood too fast, and her hand jerked reflexively, knocking her cup to the floor where it smashed.

The manageress looked around, and she and Caroline made eye contact. There was a cloud of puzzlement on the manageress's face, then she pieced together who Caroline was, and why she looked so distressed. '*Merde...!*' she said.

7.

The answer to the conundrum of Caroline's non-appearance for lunch came to Rod in a flurry of horripilation as he discarded his ski boots in the chalet hallway and padded up the stairs in thick ski socks. Caroline had met Sabine, and Sabine had told her about their tryst; Caroline had then gone back to the chalet and committed suicide; Rod would discover her corpse when he opened their bedroom door.

No, no, he said to himself. It can't be that bad...But it wasn't far off.

All of Caroline's things had gone: her Rossignol bag and makeup case from the floor; her jeans, blouses and socks from the chair; and her moisturising cream and alarm clock from the bedside table. Only Rod's things remained – juxtaposed with emptiness. He flung open the wardrobe and that too was the same: his side was full and hers void. A weakness came over him, a slipping and subsiding inside. He started to pose the question in his head when he noticed a slip of Caroline's pale green Filofax paper on the bed. With great trepidation, he picked it up.

> Your French slut isn't very discreet –
> n'est ce pas? I've taken the car and
> driven home. Enjoy the rest of the
> holiday – and the rest of your life.

Rod sat on the bed feeling blank and detached; his head was spiralling off like a released helium-filled balloon. So, Sabine *did* tell her? Or somebody did...What does it matter? She knows! That's the important thing...

In the face of this drastic development, he just wanted to turn and flee. It was too big a situation to handle, too impossible to begin to address. He got up from the bed and paced the room dementedly. Lack of a forward direction was bringing him towards panic, he realised. He had to go away and think this out. It was only twenty past two; he could get in a good two hours of skiing before dusk. The prospect cheered him marginally, and gave him the impetus to get out of the room.

Outside it was dull and very cold, and light snow continued to swirl. Nearing the main lift station, Rod met Norman and Marjorie coming the opposite way. The sight of their cheery, wool-wrapped faces pierced him with a kind of dread: they represented a quotidian standard against which he could measure how far he'd fallen. Exchanging pleasantries was every bit as awful as anticipated; but at least he was grateful they didn't ask the whereabouts of Caroline.

As Rod's gondola reached the top station, desolation was washing over him in waves. There was a cold burn in his lungs and throat, and pressure like increased G force was bearing down on his face and shoulders. He felt somehow that his life had actually ended and he was eking out some weird 'posthumous' existence – as a ghost who seemed real to others but not to himself. The light-heartedness of the other skiers registered as obscene to him, a sick joke, a false veneer on the fundamental chaos of things.

Swooping down the far side of the mountain, losing himself in the somnambulistic rhythms of the falling snow, Rod considered once again those few minutes of pleasure for which he was now paying such a heavy price. His senses had been delightfully ruffled and percolated; he'd tasted the corkscrew black magic of Sabine's loins, an experience beyond reason; but after it was all over, the feeling he ought not to have done it was immense. He recalled his first sight of Caroline afterwards, her profile framed in a window of their usual lunch restaurant, thoughtfully sipping a Perrier, unaware he was even watching her, let alone how he'd just transgressed. The guilt had so overwhelmed him then, he felt he deserved to die.

At the bottom end of the piste, Rod had to make a decision. Either he could head for the main chairlift and go back from whence he'd come; or he could follow a spur run and take another chairlift up the adjoining mountain, protracting his journey home.

The prospect of returning to the chalet and having to explain to the others what had happened made him wince and wither inside. He couldn't do it. Nor could he cope with the practical steps he knew he ought to be taking: booking himself a flight home, or arranging a place on a coach or the ski train. He had to be back at work Monday! Work...Home...It was all surreally distant, like the details of someone else's life, not his.

Rod chose the longer route; but the bad thoughts wouldn't be shaken off. He imagined Caroline arriving at their house in England and spontaneously making a bonfire of all his possessions – his clothes, his sports equipment, his CDs and videos...his Porsche in the garage...she might bash it and scratch it. Oh no! Caroline was sensible about most things, but she had a terrible temper when provoked. He might get back and find the locks changed – could she do that legally to a jointly-owned house? Surely not. More likely, she'd have left herself and gone back to her mother's. He would get a solicitor's letter in a week or so...

God, it was such a dreadful mess, and there was no way of putting it right. Rod had reached what his psychologist friend Jim would call an 'ontological crisis'. Rod fully understood that term now; it meant he couldn't see his way forward: like a seized car engine, his life wouldn't *go* anymore. As soon as he realised this idea wasn't theoretical, that it actually applied to *him*, a big wave of fear surged up from his stomach.

8.

Caroline stopped for a late lunch in the town at the bottom of the mountain road. By the time she'd finished the meal, she'd made the decision to retrace her steps and go back up. The snowstorm was getting really heavy now, and the prospect of going on alone struck her as hazardous. She and Rod would have to have it out sooner or later – why not sooner? Now her anger had come down slightly from its crescendo, she felt she could handle it – and she really wanted to know now what Rod thought he was playing at. And if – *when* – they had a dreadful fight and everybody in the chalet listened in, so what? She'd go down to the dinner table and announce the reason for it, if she wanted to.

Caroline ploughed out of the car park and took to a road which was fast becoming buried in white. Negotiating the first set of hairpin bends, she felt the chill of danger, and was really grateful they'd bothered to fit chains to the car's drive wheels. The journey soon became an ordeal, as worsening conditions rendered the way ahead increasingly featureless, but the fear of slowing too much and getting stranded kept her driving at a pace which felt reckless. To make it more awful still, the image of Rod and Sabine together kept rebounding off the walls of her skull with every heave of the suspension and protest of the engine.

Getting nearer, Caroline felt a soft blow to her stomach as the impending confrontation became more of a reality. Her feelings were in turmoil: a frothy anticipation of a new freedom unbound from Rod atop a churning bile soup of pain and resentment at having been victimised in this way. They couldn't go on after this, she decided. Such an obstacle was too great to surmount or remove, and she'd tell Rod that...

She peered ahead, seeing almost nothing as the blizzard battled with her poor overtaxed windscreen wipers. Would anyone be skiing in this? she wondered.

9.

The chairlift station materialised out of the whiteness, and Rod glided down to the entrance gate, through boot-top-deep powder. There were no signs of other skiers having come this way, and none were behind. In fact, Rod hadn't seen anybody for around quarter of an hour, and in that time the falling snow had become much heavier, with conditions approaching the whiteout levels of three days ago. Knowledge of isolation and doubts about the sagacity of taking this roundabout route were fuelling Rod's anxiety; but now there was no choice other than to go up in order to get back.

Ascending, aware that all the chairs in front were empty, as were those behind, Rod wondered if the lift operative should have stopped him – or at least warned him – from going ahead. Hardly. It was his job to see the lift worked properly and passes were valid, not to arbitrate over skiing conditions. That was the function of the piste patrolmen. Would there be any up top, to guide him back? Unlikely.

The higher Rod got the thicker the snow became; great swatches of it circulated about him, and he shivered despite his many thermal layers, double gloves and balaclava. It had to be minus-ten or minus-twelve up here, he reckoned. Again and again, he looked behind – as if previously empty chairs could be filled magically with skiers in mid-ascent. If he saw just one other skier, either in front or behind, it would convince him he wasn't being totally foolhardy. But no. The feint greyness of the top came into view, and Rod felt both excited and more profoundly scared than ever.

White, utter white, complete white, more total white than ever before, greeted Rod as he carved a path out of the station exit. His first reaction was to laugh at the novelty of it, as he'd done in the blizzard three days before. His fear – and perhaps his grip on reality itself – was loosening up. He felt careless, anarchic, a little crazy.

This whiteout was good, he decided, just what he needed. A little oblivion, a thrill-out, a flirt with the nebulous edge of experience – before facing his predicament, getting down to business and sorting through the chaos of his personal life. It wasn't a bad run, a long red which skirted Death Valley and terminated at the back of the home mountain, leaving one more gondola upwards and then a ski into the village. He'd done the run four or five times before, and had had no trouble. There's no need to chicken, he intoned. His skill would see him succeed.

From here he was pushed up into a kind of ecstasy as he surfed on through the virgin powder, the cottonwool, candyfloss nothingness, believing he'd really left his problems behind – a child's pretence reified by the unique sensory dynamics of the whiteout. And then he realised that all along he'd wanted this; he'd planned it at a level below full consciousness. Having sampled the escapist magic three days before, he'd known this was the only antidote: white oblivion, a return to the white womb. Yes! If he were a philosopher, he'd write a treatise on the dialectics of the whiteout, a much-neglected area of study indeed.

Happily motoring on, Rod connected with a particularly

deep build-up of powder which slapped right up against his chest and made his skis slew and his body careen heavily, so that he nearly fell over. '*Shee-it!*' he said. He had better be careful. And for the first time since leaving the station, he looked back and saw equal white nothingness to that which lay in front and to the sides.

He felt he'd been functioning as though in a dream, but was now coming out of it and realising this was for real. The former fear galloped back, leading an army of emergency re-actions. Just like three days ago, the wonder of the snowstorm was giving way to anxiety, and instantaneously Rod saw the flipside of white sensory deprivation. How could he be sure he was going the right way, following the run? He'd seen no piste markers, and wouldn't know if he'd drifted off. This was a very lonely part of the ski area; there were large ungroomed sections which led nowhere, and if he missed the way he could end up at the bottom of a liftless valley...And no one knew he was here...He could freeze to death before they even bothered to start looking...

Fighting the encroaching panic, Rod experimented with steering, trying to locate the gentlest gradient as he reck-oned this had to indicate the likely flow of the run. But quickly he found this to be a useless discipline. Without longer references, immediate gradient didn't mean a thing. He could be circling away from the run for all he knew. And the powder was steadily deepening around him; it was almost up to crotch level in places.

In a terrifying flash of insight, Rod saw the full extent of his error. He'd just had a severe emotional upset, and his ability to evaluate risk, his normal faculties of judgement, simply weren't functioning properly. His life with Caroline was in ruins, probably wrecked beyond recovery; and the feeling was his *whole* life, physical part included, was jeopard-ised. Like a drowning man seizing the person closest, that ruined life had latched on and was dragging him down...down into white encapsulation, white suffocation, white death.

This can't happen! Rod thought. The thought was too

loud, its desperation menacing. As the white tide reached his waist, he felt ready to renounce his atheism and start praying.

But before Rod could commence, events started to rapidly worsen. The slope fell away very sharply, and he was propelled downwards – flying almost – through a surf of chest-deep powder. Terror mangled his stomach and sensation ballooned into eidetic slow motion. Plummeting without restraint, Rod tipped to one side, felt his left leg being cruelly wrenched and saw his left ski windmill away, as his right ski, still attached, appeared above his head. Then he was free falling – jack-knifing – and perceptions of peril assaulted him in great hard nuggets, reducing him to childlike scale and helplessness.

Next thing he collided with a new surface of snow and cleaved deep down into it, like a toy soldier being pressed down by purposeful boy fingers. Then more snow fell on him like a door slamming hard on his back. As soon as there was a hiatus, he tried to move his legs and couldn't. His hips, his whole lower body was locked in position; but he knew he wasn't paralysed because he could flex his toes inside his ski boots. Meanwhile he was making swim motions against the white engulfment, trying hopelessly to maintain a pathway between his face and air.

God, this is horrible! he thought; and in the still centre of freshly erupting panic, of utter disbelief that events could *still* be worsening, he had a vision of his love for Caroline as a perfect thing which couldn't be touched by any external vicissitudes. Not by his dalliance with Sabine. Not even by his physical extinction.

10.

Caroline stood gazing into the big painted circle which marked the helicopter landing pad on the hospital roof. The storm had ceased, and the area was bathed in a crepuscular beauty of greys shading from deep to pale and then to gradated tangerine above the line of western crags.

She started crying for perhaps the eighth time now, the tears accompanied by a deep uncontrollable shuddering. Norman and Marjorie were close by, but she'd told them to let her alone unless she signalled. Without their alertness the rescue operation wouldn't have got underway nearly so quickly. If Rod lived, he'd have those two to thank...

Caroline fought a further rush of tears, and had a reaction feeling akin to the chaos of madness. She directed it at Rod, cursing him and saying in her head: *This is what you get when you take things too far, Rod. You end up waiting for helicopters on top of hospitals!* She covered her face with her scarf and blubbered helplessly, seeing visions of funerals, the faces of Rod's parents hearing the news, the rest of her life as a widow without him.

Soon the helicopter reappeared, like some dreadful insect messenger of cosmic doom. They must have found something, Caroline reasoned, otherwise they'd continue at least till it got fully dark. As the awesome machine came in to land, Caroline fixated hard on the epic pulse of its rotor thwacking the refrigerated air, trying to keep at bay the dread of what might come next. Then she made out the form of Rod in the back, evidently alive, shrouded in glittering space blankets like an over-large item of poultry.

The doors slid open and the crew emerged. With their bone-domed and visored heads, they became for Caroline the protagonists of some soulless cyberpunk future-world operating in dreamtime. She pushed past them to get to Rod, and one said, 'It's alright. He's okay,' while another added in French, '*He was very lucky.*' She peered down at Rod, and his laser-blue eyes peered back at her out of a face turned to ash, its responses slowed to the vanishing point.

'Why...?' Caroline said tremulously, not sure if she was referring to the Sabine incident, the skiing recklessness or both simultaneously. 'Y-Y-You're such a fool...' she added, Rod's image wavering and blurring beyond the thickening lenses of tears.

'I know,' Rod said in a weak throaty voice, more spirit than human. 'That became clear somewhere back there. Maybe that was when you turned back...'

'Maybe...' Caroline put her arms around his neck and pressed her face to his, absorbing some of its meat-freezer coldness. She doubted she would ever absorb all of it, but not to try seemed to her fainthearted, and that was a quality which didn't figure in her character at all.

THE EMPTY CHAIR:

Chapter 1.

As a filmmaker, Steve Penhaligon was hypersensitive to what one might call 'movie moments', those fortuitous coincidences and happy occurrences of serendipity which drive a plot along and conveniently untangle conflicts, leading to neat – perhaps too neat – resolutions. Within movies themselves, such moments seem contrived, precisely because they are contrived – coins in the currency of scriptwriting – but when they occur in *real life* then the effect is altogether different, one of awe and occult fascination, coupled with the sense that the universe is really more mysterious than we imagine, and Jungian Synchronicity is real, part of the essential magic that underpins our existences but only rarely reveals itself.

Such a 'movie moment' took place in the real life of Steve Penhaligon long, long ago, back before the age of ubiquitous mobile phone-and-computer use, the Internet and quirky techno-crises such as the Millennium bug. The moment took the form of an astounding 'coincidence', 'synchronicity', or what you will, involving…well…you can probably guess… empty chairs. The two parts were separated by a few weeks, and the first instalment unfolded at a Bonfire Night party that Steve attended with friends and TV industry colleagues at a large rented house in Redland, Bristol – and that alone proved to be epoch-making in its own right.

So, fireworks of the literal and metaphorical kind went off that night, and the event came to acquire great significance for Steve, becoming crowned as a watershed moment, one that not only marked the beginning of a redefining of his life, but also his creativity and eventually his career.

* * * *

Everything got going with an enormous bang when Guy, an assistant film editor who was a bit of a nutcase, lit a mortar out in the back garden. It went off in an ear-shattering blast of blue smoke, sending an illuminated ball thirty or forty feet vertically into the night. 'Fifteen quid each they cost!' Guy declared, giggling with the exuberance of a young child, and everyone laughed in response, relieved that it was over and agreeing it was worth the expenditure. The noise left Steve's ears clanging, reminding him of the prog rock concerts of his youth with their killer amplification.

Steve was smoking a joint, which he handed to film editor Chris as they exchanged a smile in the aftermath of the mortar's excitement. Everyone was drifting towards the bonfire, an impressive wigwam of old timber, garden waste and assorted domestic junk, now beginning to heat up and produce some sustained flame from within its smoky pall. Party hosts Chris and his girlfriend Suzy were moving house and they were using the fire as an opportunity to get rid of any unwanted junk that they might otherwise leave out for the dustman or take to the tip. Presently Suzy re-appeared from the kitchen doorway, her arms laden with a cardboard box full of old Sunday supplements, which she flung into the fire's heart.

'Perfect fuel,' Suzy said. Then she tugged at Chris's sweatshirt. 'Come on you! Give us a hand. There's loads more to get rid of.'

Chris flicked the roach into the fire, flashed Steve a smile and followed Suzy inside. Steve's gaze was drawn towards the main focus of the gathering, where Guy was now dispatching the regular fireworks. He hopped around, making his barking laugh like a bony court jester, his skull face gothic-looking in the flickering light. Steve watched as he set off an expensive roman candle. The successive showers of sparks and dancing veils of colour registered as a performance, beautiful beyond reason, flooding Steve's heart with sweet nostalgia and unearthing memories and feelings from that very early part of his life when fireworks were one of the most magically exalted things. Yes, he'd had two joints and was stoned enough to recognise the symptoms, and what was more he was enjoying himself. Dare he build on this sensation with a third?

Steve had not been smoking much at all lately, because it tended to set off or amplify the anxiety that had been a feature of his life for the last three or four years. Getting stoned had become a dangerous activity akin to Russian roulette or walking in a minefield; but tonight it felt all right, like the old days of smoking when it was just a carefree pleasure…

Yes, I'll risk it, he decided.

In the kitchen he helped himself to a glass of Weston's scrumpy and carried it into the lounge, which had been set up for a disco later in the evening. The room was empty apart from Rolf's '70s retro disco ensemble and a couple of old battered hardwood dining chairs. Chris and Suzy had sold most of their unwanted older furniture prior to the move, but seemingly no one wanted these relics of grandpa's days. Steve sat down in one of the chairs and prepared a joint, using king-size Rizlas, a mild Silk Cut cigarette and the block of resin – some particularly strong Red Lebanese he'd scored from a new source at the university.

Sitting there, he glimpsed himself as a seasoned doper – thirty-one now – going through a ritual done a million times before, and doing it with practised ease. He still retained the look of earlier years, with a tight leather jacket and jeans drawn over his tall thin frame, together with the curling, domed over-the-ears hairstyle favoured by 1960s pop stars – such as Marc Bolan and Syd Barrett – and retained by its aficionados into the '80s, in order to stave off the appearance of middle age.

The only other person in the room was Rolf, who was carrying out a sound check on the disco. He dropped the needle on the Rolling Stones *Brown Sugar*, and those familiar opening chords thundered through the speakers far too loud and Rolf killed the volume.

'Hey, that's the second time tonight I've been deafened!' Steve shouted jovially.

'*Sa-arry*,' said Rolf.

Steve crumbled quite a lot, maybe too much, of the Red

120

Leb into the joint. He knew that if he smoked most of it himself then it would take him a lot further than in recent times, and that familiar butterflies sensation started up. A big swig of cider served as the antidote to that. He was getting adept at this post-anxiety juggling act with the balls of alcohol and tetrahydrocannabinol. Dope to transport you up and cider to quell the flight phobia and take the edge off the ascent. He also had some extra diazepam on him in case of emergencies. The whole thing was just like flying, he considered, the different substances acting as engines, ailerons and rudders to provide lift, thrust and direction in just the right quantities. He lit the joint and smoked about half, then gave Rolf a turn and took the rest outside to finish by himself.

They were setting off the residual fireworks now, the little ones, the boring ones, the unloved ones, with Guy providing suitable disparaging commentary. Steve took in their scalding pinks and flashbulb blues, impossibly vivid to his stoned retinas. Suddenly his heart started to beat fast and hard like a bass drum, shaking his body to its foundations. Everything was getting faster. Next thing his whole psyche reared up on its hind legs and pushed him through a kind of hymen onto a New Level. Up here all his thoughts and perceptions linked and cross-referenced in weirdly significant ways, circulating and recycling like a pinball game turned into a fairground ride, turned into a journey of space exploration. Alongside these sensations stood the twin pillars of Fear and Delight, constant as ever, the *yin* and *yang* of being out of your tree. Steve accepted their reality, and with this acceptance came an influx of peace and the recognition that he'd passed an important test.

Whey! hey! hey! I'm stoned again, and isn't it gre-eaatt!? Always the same but always different…

Steve sauntered back to the bonfire, still going well with the addition of what looked like old skirting boards. The metaphor of fire came out strongly with the enhanced perception…the destroyer…the consumer…the cleanser… Appropriately he started to play Arthur Brown's 'Fire' in his head, the music synchronizing with the complex patterning of flame motion.

Steve heard a noise and saw Chris coming up, carrying the two battered dining chairs from the disco room. He tossed one high onto the mount of flaming boards, where it turned upside down and fell into the central inferno; the other he planted upright in the front of the fire, where it stood facing them, projecting an odd inquisitorial air, so Steve thought.

'What! You're burning the friggin' furniture too?' he said.

'Why not? Everything must go. Don't want to take it with us. Cremate it is what I say!'

Chris walked off with a chuckle, leaving Steve to study the art of combustion as applied to a chair. The flames curled around the feet, timidly at first, then sent long shooting caresses up the legs, which merged with other expeditions along the edges of the seat, the support struts and up the back, silhouetting the chair shape against a greater intensity of localised flame. He half turned as an unknown girl walked up, stood next to him and watched the burning chair as though it was the TV. She was petite and foxy with short blonde hair and a beret. Steve felt an immediate affinity with her.

'If you had to put someone in that burning chair,' he said, 'who would it be?'

'My mother,' the girl replied. She said it spontaneously and with total assurance, as though for all of her life she'd been planning to do that very thing.

Steve gave an appropriate knowing laugh. 'Yes. The same-sex parent is always the difficult one.'

'Yeah too true…'

She tailed off and together they watched the next episode in the drama of the combusting chair. By now the raffia work of the seat was well alight, with individual little flames sprouting up side by side like candle flames on a birthday cake.

'How about you?' the girl continued.

'Eh?'

'Who would you put in the chair?'

'Well…' Steve said, taking his time though he knew there could only be one possible candidate. 'It would have to be my father, wouldn't it? Who else?'

He looked back and with hallucinatory ease he projected the image of Harry Penhaligon, his dear old dad, into the chair. Who else? Harry sat impassively as the flames enveloped his tall frame, now sagging a bit at the shoulders as befits a man of sixty-four. He was wearing a grey cardigan over a sport shirt with flannel trousers and slippers – the uniform of a retired man. His paler grey hair was thin on top, wispy, with just a few strands at the front now, pushed to one side. But the gaze was the same one as he used to give Steve as a child, its severity undiminished by the decades, ice-blue eyes boring him with disapproval through the large frames of his glasses…

What are you up to this time, Steve? What's your game – putting me in a fire like this?

Steve started to giggle at the excellence of this stoned fantasy. What fitting retribution for the old git! It had both a satisfying medieval atavism and a certain aesthetic grace. What's more it was the product of a tendency that had been brewing for some time – putting his dad in the hot seat and making him answer for his misdeeds. It had developed through the period of anxiety and depression, a further stage on in the process – the searching for reasons and causes of the state and the apportioning of blame and guilt; and inevitably the consideration of the myriad possibilities for retribution. And here on this night the ideal solution to that crime-and-punishment equation had spontaneously presented itself! It had to be a sign, he thought, laughing inside…

Burn, Dad, burrnnn…Burn forever…I hate you, I hate you, I hate you…

In Steve's mental theatre, Arthur Brown concurred, manically condemning Steve's dad to his hellfire fate.

Harry was now incandescent as a column of flame passed right through the seat of the chair and through his body, swirling all around him, reducing him to a transparent spectre. He was a defunct king on a burning throne – he was overthrown! Then the dope in Steve's system surged and everything speeded up, and all sorts of ideas and memory fragments were drawn together from many disparate quarters. He felt a cosmic rush and in glorious stoned quadraphonic he got the full horror of what his dad had done to him.

Ye-ess, let him burn, let him suffer…Give him back the pain…

*But wait…*countered a more appeasing voice. *There's supposed to be another way. Remember?*

'Oh yes,' Steve said aloud.

He came back to himself and looked around. The blonde girl was gone, the fireworks had finished and the disco had started up inside. Rolf was playing 'Hi Ho, Silver Lining'.

Oh no, Steve thought. *Not that!* But even then he had a strong inkling that what he'd just experienced somehow would have life-changing significance.

For more information on *The Empty Chair* please visit:
www.rogerkeen.com/the-empty-chair.php

Roger Keen is the author of two novels, *The Empty Chair* and *Literary Stalker*, and the non-fiction works *Man of Letters* and *The Mad Artist: Psychonautic Adventures in the 1970s*. He has also written numerous short stories, articles and reviews, often with surreal or countercultural leanings, appearing in magazines and websites such as *Psychedelic Press*, *International Times*, *Reality Sandwich*, *The Digital Fix*, and *The Oak Tree Review*. During his career in film and TV, he has contributed to many award-winning dramas and documentaries for the BBC, ITV and Channel 4 – his programmes have won Royal Television Society, Worldfest-Houston and other awards. In addition, he makes short films and writes booklet essays for Blu-ray releases of classic weird and psychedelic movies.

Praise for Roger Keen's previous books:

'[*The Mad Artist* is] a significant addition to the canon of psychedelic literature.' — Leaf Fielding, author of *To Live Outside the Law*

'The whole story is a delight from beginning to end.' — William J Booker, author of *Trippers*

'I highly recommend this book to anyone with an interest in psychedelics, good writing and the human condition.' — Robert Dickins, Editor-in-Chief, *Psychedelic Press*

'[O]ne of the best UK drug memoirs, highly recommended.' — Professor Harry Sumnall, Liverpool John Moores University

'[A] dazzling, intelligent and ambitious quest to cut through conventional ways of looking at the world that ultimately yields impressive and potentially life-changing results.' — Noel Megahey, *Digital Fix* reviewer

'I really enjoyed *Literary Stalker*. It's pacy, unpredictable and often very, very funny...' — M.R. Mackenzie, author of *In the Silence* and *The Shadow Men*

'Suspenseful, impeccably researched, grisly, with judicious helpings of macabre humour, I relished this Russian doll story-within-a-story.' — Simon Clark, author of *The Night of the Triffids* and *Vampyrrhic*

'Throughout the book, Keen aptly skewers both the act of writing and the business of writing so accurately that I found myself simultaneously snickering aloud and squirming in my chair whilst reading it, which works perfectly for something one might call a metafiction thriller.' — David Dubrow, author of *The Armageddon Trilogy* and *The Appalling Stories Series*

'A major question you will be confronted with over the course of this book is going to be where fantasy ends and reality begins.' — Chad A. Clark, author of *Winward* and *Yesterday, When We Died*

'This is quite a wickedly written book where at times I just didn't know if it was a story in a story or actually happening.' — Susan Hampson, *Books From Dawn Till Dusk*

'Ideal for fans of both comedic and suspense thrillers, the novel proudly wears its influences on its bloody sleeve and succeeds.' — Josh Hancock, *Morbidly Beautiful*

'Keen could have taken the easy route and written this as a straightforward novel with a linear narrative, but Keen isn't your average writer, and his use of a story-within-a-story multidimensional narrative is more than just a gimmick, it takes the reading experience into a whole new level of cleverness.' — Jim Mcleod, *Ginger Nuts of Horror*

'*The Empty Chair* is utterly compelling, particularly the intriguing descriptions of the film- and television-making process. I found it to be a page-turner. I wanted to follow Steve through the twists and turns of his life. I was fascinated and invested.' — Terry Grimwood, author of *Joe* and *The Last Star*

'*The Empty Chair* is a big book, in more ways than one. Above all it's big in its ambition and most impressively, it's hugely successful in achieving what it sets out to do.' — Noel Megahey, *To The Last Page*

'The subject of dementia is beautifully handled, incorporating that dark humour which tends to be shared between family members in difficult situations, and the inevitable giggling when the alternative is tears...' — Jules Lucton

'[*The Empty Chair* has] probably the most remarkable ending to any novel that I have ever read, one I could not put down today. So emotional, so spiritual, so utterly Jungian and Proustian.' — Des Lewis, *The Gestalt Real-Time Reviews*

More information on: **www.rogerkeen.com**